The Four Before Me

Copyright © 2019 by E. H. Night

Printed in the United States of America

First Printing, 2019

THE
FOUR
BEFORE
ME

E. H. NIGHT

To those who cheered me on, even though I had specifically said to be quiet so I could write.

Prologue

Susan placed her warm earmuffs snugly around her head and walked along the railroad tracks. Though it was almost spring, the evening air was still chilly. She hugged herself as she picked up speed. Her footsteps soon tapped in tandem with the rhythmic chugging of an approaching train. The vibrations worked themselves up her already-rickety ankles like vines, begging her to wake from her daze, but she paid no attention to them. The tracks started to shake even harder beneath her feet, causing her to finally stumble. She collected herself and continued on as if there had been no interruption at all. The chugging turned into whistling, and she whistled a little tune in return. She kept her eyes focused on the sun setting before her as the train hissed in the rear like a territorial cat, warning her to move out of its way.

Susan closed her eyes and stopped walking. A buttery smile spread across her elderly lips, and the evidence of many decades-worth of laughter appeared on her face in the form of deep lines and wrinkles. With freckles indiscernible from age spots, she wore her years like fine jewelry. They were something to be envied.

The train hissed even louder, offering one final warning, but Susan ignored its suggestion. In one screeching halt, it transformed her flesh and bones into a beautiful ruby — one without a price-tag, one that couldn't be returned.

Chapter 1

"Just Like Starting Over"

April 4th, 1988

Alice arrived in Wintersburg to see the movers unloading her furniture from a rusted van. Her grandmother's sudden passing was still on her heart, but she made a great effort to keep a smile on her face. This was a time to be strong. She carried a few bags into the house from her car and placed them on the kitchen counter. Her hands trembled as the scent of her grandmother's heavy perfume seeped out and filled the air, forcing her to push back a few loose tears. The small amount of optimism that she conjured allowed her to pause for a moment and gain a new appreciation for the rental home. She decided that she had made the right choice by leaving Parkington. After all, there hadn't really been many better options. She'd been paying month-to-month for a while and had no real reason to stay in the city. Without any family left, she was bound to nothing.

Once her bags had been emptied onto the counter top, she decided to take a quick look around to see what items she needed the most. While driving through Wintersburg, she had taken notice of a little local grocery store that was only a few blocks away from the house. She figured that it would be nice to go for a walk to absorb some of the sounds and scents of the small town. Even though she hadn't been sleeping or eating well for a few days, she knew that a trip to the store was still necessary. There wasn't a single edible item among her belongings, and places like Wintersburg didn't have late-night restaurants available if she happened to get hungry later.

Alice grabbed her pair of moving shoes again and placed them clumsily upon her feet, not even bothering to untie the laces before shoving each foot inside. Despite the sunny sky, the air was deceptively harsh and cold, so she bundled herself up in an over-sized sweater, and grabbed her favorite jean jacket for good measure. She sighed heavily as she looked around the kitchen one final time.

"Did they even consider cleaning this place before renting it out?" she thought while shaking her head in disbelief. *"For heaven's sake, there's still a few dried up slices of pizza in the fridge."* Alice turned to the wobbly bar-stool across from the counter and reached for her purse. "Well, at least it's cheap," she said aloud.

She slung the purse across her shoulder and jingled her keys like a broken wind chime as she made her way to the front door. Taking more care than what was needed, she locked it behind herself and jiggled the handle back and forth a few times before she finally headed toward the sidewalk. City life had left its mark upon her. From her haircut to her mannerisms, it was obvious that she wasn't a local. There was a visible amount of fear in her movements and a difference in how she presented herself. Her nails were polished a bright pink color, her jean jacket was intentionally faded, and her blue jeans hugged her figure as if they'd been professionally tailored specifically for her shape. These clothes definitely were not bought from the secondhand store across town.

The patchy brown grass was oddly more inviting than the florescent green turf that she had been used to seeing in Parkington. The air was cleaner here, the skies were bluer, the people were... fewer. She could only trust that everyone was just as friendly as her grandmother had often told her when she would sit and reminisce about her younger years. Hopefully, things hadn't changed much since then. Alice recalled the many tales that she'd heard about the younger folks. She thought it was so exciting to hear about the girls secretly putting on lipstick, everyone swimming at night in the lake, and all of the other types of innocent trouble that people seemed to find themselves in. There was excitement in the simplicity of it all.

As she moved along the sidewalk, she resembled a runway model, sauntering with perfectly-spaced steps, one shifting directly in front of the other. Even though Alice seemed to exude a great deal of confidence, she was surprisingly more insecure than most women her age. She had simply been a fan of the latest trends, and her occupation required it. Thanks to a few phone calls, she'd been able to confirm that there was a little salon in town, and she was planning on speaking with the owner the following morning. With the growing demand of perms and fluffy bangs, even in tiny communities, she was confident that she'd be able to find work locally. Even though she was going to miss her old boss and her regular clientele, life was guiding her down a new path, and she hadn't once considered resisting its call. She was young, she was attractive, and she was all alone in the world. A combination like that could either create a wonderful opportunity or a complete and utter disaster — or perhaps even both. Only time would tell which path she'd end up taking.

***

Alice stood in front of the local grocery store, Medley's. Among the assortment of sun-faded vending machines, she noticed a bulletin board hanging in the shade underneath the awning. There were various hand-written listings for an assortment of things — from expired yard sales to free kittens, various lawn-mowing services, and so on. Most importantly, there was a pristine flyer in the top center of the board with the faces and names of four women photocopied onto it. Clearly, someone had cared about this flyer enough to staple new ones on top of the old ones each time they had gotten wrinkled or had been torn from the unpredictable weather. Alice let her thumb run along the ruined pages as if she were casually shuffling through a deck of cards. Her thumb stopped on the top flyer and she read each word with a growing curiosity.

Missing

Four women have been reported missing from Wintersburg since 1985.

At this time, it is unknown if the cases are related, or if any foul play was involved.

If you have information leading to the location or happenings of any of these women, please contact Detective Darrow at the local police station. You are allowed to remain anonymous if you wish.

Alice read the names and examined the faces of each woman.

Jessica Roberts, aged 31 at the time of her disappearance. Was last seen leaving

Medley's on September 27th, 1985. She is believed to have been wearing a red jacket with large buttons, blue jeans, and red canvas shoes. Brown hair. Brown eyes. Tattoo of a rose on her ankle.

Ashley Culver, aged 24 at the time of her disappearance. Was last seen walking through the Wintersburg Cemetery on June 14th, 1986. She is believed to have been wearing a gray t-shirt, hot pink running shorts, and white athletic shoes. Brown hair. Hazel eyes. No known tattoos or distinguishing markings.

Tammy Thomas, aged 27 at the time of her disappearance. Was last seen at Kirt's Pub on October 17th, 1987. She is believed to have been wearing a purple sweater, light blue jeans, and silver flat shoes. Brown hair. Hazel eyes. No known tattoos or distinguishing markings.

Sarah Noe, aged 21 at the time of her disappearance. Was last seen in front of her home on Fifth Street, on February 16th, 1988. She is believed to have been wearing a jean jacket, dark blue jeans, and brown ankle boots. Brown hair. Brown eyes. No known tattoos.

Alice shuddered from a sudden cold chill that tickled her across the back of the neck. She wondered what could have happened to all of the women in such a short amount of time. Surely it couldn't have been just a coincidence. She adjusted her slipping purse strap and headed inside the store. A new sense of worry and dread filled her veins, and anxiety bloomed within her like an unwanted dandelion. She forced herself to push through the tension and tried to recall the mental list of things that she had intended on purchasing.

"Cleaning spray — probably a few bottles of that, paper towels, light bulbs, and something simple for dinner," she thought. *"I'll be in and out of here quickly. I can always come back later with the car if I really need to."*

Alice grabbed the items as quickly as she could, almost knocking over a display of canned goods, and briskly walked to the cash register. The male cashier greeted her with an unenthusiastic "hello" and was met with Alice's singsongy voice in return.

"Hi, how's your day going... um..." she squinted to see his name tag. "... Jim!" she exclaimed.

Taken aback by her enthusiasm, Jim looked up from the items and met her eyes. "It's okay, I guess. I've had better and I've had worse," he replied. "So, I don't think I recognize you. Are you new in town or something, or are you just passing through?"

"Oh, I just moved here. I guess you probably don't get too many new faces in a place like this, do you?" she asked.

Jim scanned through her items slowly, trying to savor the conversation. His shift had been fairly uneventful and boring up until this point. "Not really, I guess. People pass through here and there, but they don't really buy these types of things. They mostly just pick up beef jerky or sodas. You know, road snacks." He fumbled with the box of light bulbs, unsure of where the price was. "So, why'd you come to Wintersburg anyway? You look more like a city chick to me."

Alice laughed. "Is it that obvious? I guess I could tone things down a bit to try to blend in a little better." She chuckled and reached into a bucket of small wrapped candies and placed a handful of them onto the counter. "So what's going on with that poster out front? Are those women all really from this area?"

"Poster? Oh! The one with the missing girls?" He asked, already knowing the answer by Alice's immediate nodding. "Yeah, that's kind of the town mystery, I guess. People are saying all sorts of things. Mostly, everyone is talking about the possibility of a serial killer on the loose. I think they're all just bored and turning something small into something bigger to have stuff to gossip about. If you ask me, those four girls just went somewhere else."

"Why would they just leave though?" Alice asked. "I'm sure they have family or people they'd miss, right?"

Jim's palms raised and motioned toward the entire building, and he shrugged. "Well, I love this town, but look around. There aren't really too many opportunities here. Younger people leave all the time, but the only difference is they usually tell someone about it first. I'm guessing that each of those girls just didn't want to deal with an interrogation from people, and decided to hitch rides with someone who was passing through. From my understanding, they weren't the most, uh, family-oriented women. I heard that it took almost two weeks for one of them to even be reported missing because she was known to stay out all the time." He gulped and wet his pale chapped lips before continuing. "I wouldn't think about it too much, but it's best to be safe. Just be kind of cautious, you know, especially since it could always be something bigger.

After all, the girls did look a lot like each other. Killers tend to have types, at least that's what I've seen on TV." He paused suddenly, and his eyes quickly widened.

"What? What is it?" Alice prodded. "Why do you look freaked out all of a sudden?"

"It's nothing. Well, I don't want to worry you too much, but you do kind of resemble them..."

"You're just trying to scare me now!" Alice retorted, giggling. "Whatever. What's the total, Jim?" She opened her wallet and sorted through a few bills.

Jim feigned a weak smile and shrugged. "Just hand me that five and get out of here," he teased, forcing himself to look as if he had been joking.

"Thanks again. I'll probably be coming back a lot over the next few weeks. I'm just buying things as I need them for now." Alice flashed a quick smile, grabbed the paper bag, and turned toward the exit.

"Take care, um, what was your name, Miss?"

"It's Alice. I'll see ya soon, I'm sure!" she called back as she left the store. She turned the corner and stopped by the bulletin board once more before starting her journey home. She looked at the faces a little longer than she had earlier and thought about what Jim had said.

"Do I really look like them?" she wondered. *"He's probably just bored and trying to mess with me for fun or something."*

She started walking again and rounded the crumbling narrow path that led back to the sidewalk. After she'd journeyed for an entire block, she felt something stuck to the bottom of her shoe. She paused and lifted her foot to examine it. "Gross!" she exclaimed in a loud whisper.

She dragged her foot along the edge of the sidewalk, trying to scrape the old piece of gum away. Shortly after succeeding, she looked up and noticed a man in the distance. He was walking along the sidewalk on the opposite side of the street but seemed to be heading in the same direction that she was going. She still felt a little jumpy and nervous from the conversation with Jim and from seeing the flyer, so she was immediately suspicious of the man. She tried to compose herself quickly and began walking again, making an effort to keep a decent amount of space between herself and the stranger. After a short while, she began to hear his footsteps trailing closely behind her.

"What? When did he cross the street?" she wondered as she increased her speed

even more.

The man's footsteps grew louder and louder, as did the beating of Alice's heart until the sounds were indiscernible from each other.

Alice ran for the rest of the two blocks until she made it to her front porch. Still panting, she dropped the paper bag in front of the door and fumbled with her keys. With extremely shaky hands, she finally got the key into the hole and turned it. She grabbed the grocery bag, slammed the door behind her, and threw her things onto the floor. She peered out of the living room window and saw the man shuffle past her house, but he didn't even pause to take notice of it or of her. Relief washed over her skin like a cool shower on a hot day, and she sank her tired body deep into the couch.

"Good grief, I'm so jumpy today," she mumbled. "I really need to start getting more sleep." She ran her hands through her hair and leaned all the way back into the cushions. They felt comforting and cool against her skin as if they were holding onto her gently. She exhaled slowly, and her pulse calmed down to a normal speed. The relief didn't last long though.

Knock Knock Knock

Alice jumped. Her heart felt like it hit her throat and plummeted into her stomach all at the same time. She crept back over to the window and peaked through the blinds once more."Oh. It's a woman," she thought, relieved that it wasn't the man she'd seen a moment ago. She walked over to the door and cracked it just enough to fully show her face to the stranger.

"Hi, neighbor! I just wanted to introduce myself," the woman began. She appeared to be around the same age as Alice, give or take just a couple of years at most. Her long hair was fiery, and she had a spray of oak-colored freckles across her cheeks and nose. Her eyes were large, green, and full of life. She resembled a tamed, combed, and plainly-dressed Cyndi Lauper. Her gentle smile was warm though, and Alice immediately noticed her friendly presence. She felt comfortable enough to open the door the rest of the way.

"I'm Tiffany, your neighbor," the girl continued while pointing to the painted yellow house next door. "I was wondering if you needed any help moving in or anything." She flashed an even larger smile, and then concern filled her eyes. "Um, are you okay? You look like you've just seen a ghost or something."

Alice returned the smile and offered up a friendly response. "It's nice to meet you. I'm Alice. And yeah, sorry if I seem a little skittish. I'm probably just stressed from being in a new place." She stepped to the side. "Here, come in."

Tiffany offered a nod and stepped through the door, immediately looking all around. "Wow. It looks the same. The paint is still chipping in the corner, and everything..." she said, allowing her thoughts to trail off.

"Yeah, I'm not sure what happened. The landlord, Roger, said he was going to clean this place up before I got here, but it looks like he never got around to it."

"That's Roger for ya. He has the best intentions, but he always forgets to go through with things. You have to nag him to get anything done on time," Tiffany replied.

"Oh, darn. I wish I'd known that before!" She smiled and looked past the dining area, toward the kitchen. "I didn't get much from the grocery store, or I'd offer you something to drink."

"Actually!" Tiffany began. "I brought some things over for you." She walked into the kitchen, clearly very familiar with the house's layout, and began unpacking her backpack onto the counter, placing several items down. "I hope you like these. If not, don't feel obligated to keep them or anything," she said, ending each sentence with a smirk. "Here! Let's have some hot cocoa!"

"Wow, you didn't need to do all of this!" Alice exclaimed. "Thank you so much!"

Tiffany was already rummaging through a cabinet by the time Alice had finished speaking. She grabbed two mugs and began rinsing them out into the sink.

Alice was surprised. "You seem to really know your way around," she said.

Tiffany filled the mugs with water and placed them into the microwave. She confidently pressed a few buttons and turned to face Alice once more. "Well, I probably should explain that. Sorry. I didn't mean to just help myself around your place. It's a habit, I guess." She opened the box of cocoa and pulled out two packets. "A close friend of mine lived here right before you. We would always come here after our shifts at the restaurant to just relax and hang out together."

"Oh, that makes sense. Why did she move out? She left so many of her things behind. The cabinets are still full of her dishes and everything."

Tiffany sighed and tightened her lips for a moment as if she was trying to come up with the right words to say, but a loud series of beeping sounds interrupted her thought process. She walked over the microwave, removed the hot mugs of water, and brought them back to the counter. As she opened the packets of cocoa, she offered up more information. "Sarah didn't exactly move out. Or maybe she did. No one really knows what happened for sure. She was just gone one day." Tiffany's words paused and she poured the packets into each mug.

"Sarah... Hmm..." Alice said slowly as if trying to recall something. "Wait. Sarah? The one from the Missing Poster at the store?" She spat out in disbelief. "The one on the bulletin board?"

Tiffany weakly nodded and retrieved a small spoon from a drawer. The clanking of metal against the porcelain caused a vein to throb in her forehead and her pleasant aura dimmed for a brief moment. "I wish I knew what really happened. She wasn't the type to just run off like that. She would have told me if she had been making plans to leave. We trusted each other with everything, even our darkest secrets." She stopped stirring the cocoa and scooted one of the mugs toward Alice. "I wouldn't worry about it too much though. In a small town like this, people tend to get carried away with rumors. One time, half of the population thought the baker in Medley's was a vampire just because he liked to take walks at night. Sure, he was a little pale, but that's kind of what happens when you're inside working all day. He rarely got out to see the sun." She pushed out a little snorty chortle and took in a slow chocolatey sip. Her eyes couldn't mask the worry though. "I'm sure nothing too crazy is going on. I hope not, anyway."

A weak smile formed on Alice's lips, but her eyes reflected Tiffany's concern. "Yeah, hopefully, it's all just gossip."

Chapter 2

"Steel Magnolias"

Alice awoke the next morning to hear the sounds of birds chirping. Their high-pitched songs offered up a little hope that the warmth of spring would soon be in the air. She wiped the sleep from her eyes with the back of her hands, and let out a long yawn before sitting upright in her bed. Yesterday's clothes had been tossed in a messy pile on the floor, and she carelessly added last night's pajamas on top of them before making her way over to the bathroom.

"Today is going to be a good day," she assured herself as she turned the handle for the shower. *"I was able to get a full night's sleep this time. What could go wrong?"*

The sounds of trapped air escaping from the water pipes hit Alice like a train. Startled, she jumped backward, slipped on the floor mat, and fell against the bathroom cabinet behind her. The impact from the fall caused the clay toothbrush holder to tumble over and shatter onto the tile, sending tiny sharp pieces all around the room. Taking care to avoid stepping on anything dangerous, she stood up and tip-toed out of the bathroom and into the living room. She headed in the direction of the kitchen where she had noticed a broom propped up near the back door over there when she'd first moved her things in. She grabbed it, along with the dustpan, and entered the bathroom once more. As she swept, she noticed a few long brown hairs on the floor beside the cabinet.

"I wonder if these are Sarah's too," she thought. *"They look like they're a few inches too long to be mine. They have to be hers, or someone else's."*

Alice continued sweeping and noticed a much more sizable clump of hair — probably about ten or fifteen strands stuck together, near the hinge of the bathroom door. She bent down and picked the bundle up, dropping the broom down beside her. The hairs had their dried fleshy bulbs still attached at the roots as if they had been pulled out in one single forceful tug. Alice sprinkled them onto the floor where they dispersed quickly, much like the clay shards had before. She finished sweeping, emptied the dustpan, and finally began her shower. She wasn't going to let her mind wander again today. She'd spent too much of the previous day wandering around like an anxious mess, and there were too many things left to accomplish. Besides, was a single clump of hair really that much of a concern? As a hairdresser, she'd seen the hinges of curling irons tear ribbons of hair out from people's scalps many times before. A few stray strands shouldn't have been much of a concern or surprise, especially in a bathroom.

After her shower, she quickly threw on some clothes, grabbed her black suit jacket, and slid into her favorite pair of bright pink pumps. Despite Jim's comments about how obvious it was that she was a "city chick", she felt that it was still important to dress to impress. She'd made plans to find a job, and she knew that her appearance was as important as a portfolio in this situation.

Once her looks were squared away, she headed outside and started the car's engine. The sounds of Poison escaped from the speakers, and before she even realized it, she was singing along. She breezed through the small streets, only having to pause at a few stop signs, and found herself really admiring the lack of traffic. It was a very huge contrast to the loud horns and red lights that were always all over Parkington in the mornings. In what seemed like no time at all, she wheeled onto Main Street, and Edna's Salon appeared right in front of her. She turned the music down and quickly pulled into the gravel lot, maneuvering away from the other three cars to park alone.

Alice hurried to the entrance as she nervously fiddled with her loose pearl bracelet. Once in front of the door, she let out a long breath and stepped inside. Upon first glance, everything looked outdated. The floors were nicked, the once-white floral wallpaper was yellowed from age and tobacco smoke, causing it to lift up and curl at the edges. The only customer might as well have been asleep. Pop music played quietly from the stereo near the bathroom, which was probably just as unexciting to set eyes upon. As she examined the place further, she realized that there seemed to be a good amount of booths, especially for such a small establishment. She counted six styling chairs, three on one side in front of a long horizontal mirror, three on the other, and four hooded dryers fitted in between. She felt hopeful that the owner would have an empty spot available for her.

Alice walked toward the desk and was greeted in the distance by a small gaunt woman. The woman's short curled hair was so silver, it almost appeared to be blue. She had on a dark plum shade of lipstick that had been accidentally smudged onto her front tooth, and a full set of bright pink fake nails, which looked a lot like Alice's.

"Yeah, how can I help you?" the woman's voice called out as she approached.

"Hi, I was just wondering if you were hiring. I'm certified and have been working in Parkington as a stylist for two years. I just moved to the area yest —"

"Parkington? Why'd you come all the way out here?" the woman interrupted while placing a cigarette in between her lips. She seemed more annoyed than interested.

"Well, my grandmother passed away recently. She always talked about how she loved growing up in this town." She stopped for a second to collect her emotions. "I figured I'd move here to see what the fuss was about. I don't have any other family, so —"

"No other family?" the woman interrupted. "Who doesn't have a family? It's the 80's. Even that alien... what's his name... you know the one, from that movie with the bicycle or whatever..."

"Uh, E...T...?" Alice stammered.

"Yeah, even that weird little E.T. guy found a family. What happened to yours?"

"Well, I — I'm not really sure. I was told that my parents passed away in an accident shortly after I was born. It was just my grandmother and me until recently."

The woman's cold mannerisms changed and she looked at Alice with apologetic sympathy. She waved a small cloud of smoke away from her face and inquired further, but more politely. "Oh, I'm sorry, dear. What was your grandmother's name? You said she was from Wintersburg? In a town this small, I'm sure I'd know of her."

"Susan Foster. She said she used to —"

The woman interrupted her again. "Susan! My oh my, you're Susie's granddaughter?" She spoke with enough enthusiasm to cause the distant and tired client to look up from her book for a moment. "What happened to her? I mean, I'm sorry. That's rude of me to ask all of these questions."

Alice moved her hands back and forth in front of her. "No, no. I understand. She, well, she passed quickly. It was all very sudden."

The woman seemed satisfied with the vague answer and nodded. "Well, it's good that she didn't suffer, then. Susie never was one for lingering." She straightened her posture, inhaled another puff of smoke, and exhaled it in a long snake-like stream away from Alice. "I'm Edna, by the way. So you're here for a booth, right?"

"Yeah, if that would be okay. It doesn't seem like you need much help around here though." Her voice grew softer as she looked around at the nearly vacant salon.

"Oh, don't you worry about that. It'll pick up in about an hour. This is the only salon nearby. People flock to it like a confessional, just waiting to talk about whatever happens to be on their hearts each day. You can start today if you want. Do you already have any supplies with you?"

Alice smiled appreciatively and sat her purse on the counter. "That'd be great! I have everything I need, I think. Thank you so much! Let me just grab some things from the car."

"Hey — I'm thankful for the help. If you're anything like your grandma, then I'm sure we'll get along just fine. Consider this salon to be your new family, dear."

***

Tiffany brought out a menu for the lone man sitting in the far corner of the diner. She noticed that he seemed to be either nervous or just plain uncomfortable, and was very adamant about hiding his face from everyone. It was apparent that he was attempting to be casual and subtle about the whole thing, but other customers didn't usually sit with their heads resting on their hands and their hat bills turned down when simply placing an order for soda. He hadn't even looked up from the table. The more effort that the man had put into concealing himself, the more curious Tiffany became. She set the menu down on the table in front of him, and he mumbled a couple of words of faux appreciation.

"Thank you." His voice was a combination of a whisper and a growl as if a Tom Waits song was about to burst out of his throat at any second.

"Mm-hmm. Just wave me over when you're ready to order. I'll be wiping off some of these tables." Tiffany turned around and walked to a nearby booth. She leaned over it and began cleaning while making sure to maintain a clear shot of the man. *"Something's not right with that one,"* she thought. *"He's not even picking up the menu."*

She continued to stare from afar as she wiped the same spot over and over again, not paying attention to anything or anyone except for him. She noticed that he sat very still, almost completely motionless as he sipped from his straw until he slowly and carefully reached into his leather jacket.

"Wait... What is he doing now?" Tiffany wondered. She stopped wiping the table and blatantly gawked at the man. She watched intently as he pulled out a folded white piece of paper, opened it up, and stared at it for a brief moment before returning it back into his jacket pocket. In one swift motion, he adjusted his sleeves and raised his hand sheepishly.

Tiffany walked back toward him with hesitancy and pulled a pen and notepad from her apron. Her hands shook slightly from nervousness. "What did you decide on?" she asked in a friendly tone, trying to maintain her small-town charm.

The man handed the menu back to her. "Just the bill for the drink."

Tiffany noticed his hands as she grabbed onto the sticky plastic menu. They looked like strong hands, tough hands that had stories to tell. Riddled with cracks, his visible veins traveled across his bones like dry streams. He wore no rings or jewelry, only several large cuts across his fingers and his thumb.

"Yeah, it'll be just a dollar," she said while forcing herself to look uninterested. She continued to stare as he reached back into his jacket pocket. Only instead of the white paper that he'd pulled out a moment before, he revealed a small wad of bills and sat two of them onto the table. Tiffany picked them up, nodded, and walked back over to the table that she'd been pretending to clean. Her eyes stayed on the man until he eventually got up and left quietly through the front entrance.

"Are you okay, Tiff?" a gentle male voice said from behind her.

Tiffany jumped. "What the hell, Pat? Yeah, I'm fine. Did you — did you see that man?" she said, motioning to the table where he'd been sitting.

"I didn't pay much attention. What happened?"

"Well, nothing really. He just seemed kind of strange, I guess."

"Tiff, this is Wintersburg. Everyone who stops through here is strange," Pat said.

Tiffany's serious tone faltered and she let out a small breathy chuckle. "You're right. I probably just read him wrong or something."

"Maybe, maybe not. Did he tip?"

Tiffany nodded. "Yep, he did."

"You're right... He is a weirdo! No one ever tips around here," he said while faking a frightened expression.

Tiffany smacked him lightly on the shoulder. "Geez, stop it. I can't tell you anything."

"Whatever. Want to help us clean up a bit? Marcia left the freezer open again and now the chicken tenders are way more tender than they should be."

"Marcia, Marcia, Marcia," she said while laughing. "I guess I have no choice, do I?"

***

Tiffany sat down on the couch in front of her TV and found herself to be extremely fidgety and restless. The restaurant hadn't been terribly busy that day, but she felt especially drained after finishing her shift. There was a raw feeling in her gut, an unmistakable sense of dread, and she wasn't seeming to have any success in distracting herself from it. After repositioning the cushion behind her back several times, she finally succumbed to her restless legs' wishes and decided to take a stroll through the town.

She often found the perfect blend of excitement and calmness in her evening walks. The moon and stars chose to illuminate the most unusual things, and she was always keen on exploring what the night sky's hands held out before her. There was art in the darkness and she was always more than willing to find it. She grabbed a flashlight and a pocket knife from the kitchen drawer, just to be safe, and zipped them both safely into her messenger bag. She walked over to the back door, slid into her white canvas flats as if she was preparing to have them painted by the earth's mud, and was finally ready to begin her journey. After she had locked the door behind herself, the first breath of fresh air had already started to calm her heart.

The air was cool and refreshing against her skin and inside of her lungs. She had felt so clammy the entire day, so even the harsh breeze felt nice as it moved across her face. Her warm scarf of long red hair caught the light here and there, causing her to resemble an ember that had just escaped from a nearby fireplace. She fluttered across the sidewalk, allowing the wind to choose the path that she would take.

One block, two blocks, three, and four — She had eventually lost count of how far she'd gone and how much time had actually passed. All that mattered was she was finally feeling more relaxed, and the stress of the day had seemingly brushed itself out of her mind. She looked ahead and realized that she was getting close to the local fishing lake, and a childlike burst of curiosity filled her joints. She started to walk faster and faster until she approached the rickety fence that blocked the rest of the path that led down to the water.

"When has a fence ever stopped me before?" she asked herself with amusement. *"It'll be fine. It's not like I'm going swimming in there or anything. At least, not tonight anyway."* She looked around at the woods. The tall trees and wiry brush encompassed the entirety of the lake, gripping it protectively like a dog's teeth around a brand new tennis ball. This was Wintersburg's hidden gem — a beautiful sparkling morsel of freedom from the mundane. It was a place of first kisses, first cigarettes, and first beers; it was a place of irreplaceable memories.

She spotted something that appeared to be a little man-made trail off in the distance. At least from where she was standing, it seemed promising enough. Rather than risking a few unneeded rusty scrapes, Tiffany decided to see where the clearing would lead her instead of climbing the fence. After all, she wasn't on this walk to get into trouble or to contract something like tetanus from the rust. She just wanted to ease her mind and to take in the beauty of nature. Surely, there couldn't have been a better opportunity to do so than this one.

She turned to the left and headed down the pathway, ducking carefully below the thin branches that poked out from either side. Sticks, moss, and overgrown grass helped her to maintain a slow and careful pace for the most part. She paused briefly to reach into her bag and grabbed the flashlight. The trees' branches weren't allowing for much moonlight to trickle through, and she was struggling to see where she was actually stepping. As she pressed the button upward, the flashlight kicked on and illuminated everything in front of her. It became very apparent that no one had walked through the pathway in several months, or possibly even longer. She admired the untouched purity of nature for a moment and then ventured deeper and deeper. About thirty feet ahead of her, there seemed to be an open area. She carefully navigated the rest of the descending path.

When Tiffany reached the clearing, she realized that there was nothing more to it than that. It was just a boring clearing at the bottom of a long sloping trail. It wasn't anything to write home about, that's for sure. She turned her flashlight off and looked around at the slightly moon-lit branches. They encircled her much like the rest of the forest had encircled the lake, and she suddenly felt safe in the arms of Mother Nature. Her eyes wandered all over until she began admiring the small patch of flowers off in the distance. She walked toward them, no longer paying attention to where she was stepping.

"Flowers!" she thought. *"It's not even warm out yet. How could there be flowers out here already?"* Her excitement grew like weeds with each step, bringing her closer and closer to the prize. She was determined to pick a few to take home and put into a pretty vase. She thought that maybe, if there were enough, she could even bring some back for her new neighbor, Alice. As she crept closer, she considered that both houses could benefit from some liveliness. While she expected to be able to smell something sweet, she was expecting the scent to be more floral, and not the sickly sweet stench that was commonly associated with decay.

"It smells like something died out here," she thought before she instinctively wiped her nose onto her sleeve. The odor was almost too much for her to handle.

From clear air to peppered skies, small

corpse flies started to smack into her face. She swatted them away here and there, but they only grew thicker as she kept walking forward. They crawled through her hair and perched themselves onto the edges of her ears, buzzing angrily with hungry bellies. She frantically smacked herself in the face and all over her head repeatedly, trying desperately to scare the flies away. They were determined to find something edible on, or even inside of her.

"Stupid gnats! Go away —" she shrieked, before crouching down and spitting all over her mouth. She barely even bothered to make an attempt to wipe the twitching wing-filled drool off of her chin as she continued to flail feverishly. The corpse flies climbed the coppery fuzz in her nose like ropes, trying desperately to find any sort of entrance inside of her body. She snorted and sneezed them out while continuing to smack the air and herself. "Leave me alone!" she yelled, earning herself another seedy mouthful of the insects. They buzzed against her tongue and gums, mimicking the fizzing sensation of one of her favorite candies — Pop Rocks.

When she tried to escape the area, one of her feet became wedged inside the exposed root of a tree, and she tripped, leaving the shoe behind. She fell forward into the twig-littered dirt, which caused her to land awkwardly onto her wrist, slightly injuring it. The pain shot up through the bones in her forearm, and she cried out, earning yet another unwanted mouthful of hungry flies. They continued to pester her, speeding across her cheeks and into her eyes like pin-sized darts. She curled up into a ball, placed her hands behind her head, her face onto her knees, and sobbed. She felt hopeless. Her cries echoed out powerfully but were quickly pushed back into the clearing by the tall trees that stood all around, watching the scene from above coldly and menacingly.

In a sudden moment of clarity, she grabbed the flashlight from her bag again. With one hand, she turned it on and tossed it into the distance. In what seemed like only seconds, the flies started to scatter away, and they headed off toward the intriguing new light source. Though a few still lingered behind to lick the salty sweat and tears from her face and neck, Tiffany was able to see again. She sat upright and ran her fingers through her hair while trying to comb away the dirt and debris. As soon as her breathing calmed, she looked around for her missing shoe.

The flashlight in the distance provided a little more light to the surrounding area, and she was able to spot her canvas slipper sticking out from the tree root only a few feet away. She crawled toward it, reached forward, and let out a shriek that could have pierced the ears of any living creature near the lake that night. She fell sideways and realized that she hadn't been crawling over roots and branches at all. Rested confidently against her leg, a hand was protruding from the ground, with only enough flesh remaining to keep the bones in place. Its bare fingertips scraped and tickled against her ankle as she pulled away in horror. In front of her, the stained white shoe reflected the light as it rested securely inside the bend of a partially buried leg.

Chapter 3

"Cheers"

The sun woke Alice earlier than usual. Its rays skipped across her pores and danced along her faint smile lines for a while before it finally decided to settle itself warmly upon her long dark lashes. She opened her eyes in protest and let out a brief exaggerated yawn before turning to place her feet neatly into a pair of purple fluffy house slippers. The slippers had been gifted to her by her grandmother in December after they'd gone to see the Purple People Eater movie together. Having not known that it was supposed to be a children's movie upon arrival, they still managed to enjoy themselves. The movie had become a little bit of a joke between them from then on.

Alice sat still for a moment and found herself missing her grandmother while she stared down at the purple fluff. She'd not yet taken the time to mourn or reminisce since the cremation, and emotions were building up inside of her more and more with each passing day. Her eyes wandered across the room before they stopped to fixate on the short white vase that had been resting peacefully upon the vanity.

"Oh, Gram," she thought. *"We're finally in Wintersburg together. If you only knew..."* A small hot tear fell from one of her eyes and left a mark upon her satin pant leg. It spread like wet invisible ink across the fabric. One tear turned into two tears, and two turned into too many more to count. She broke her gaze with the urn and tilted her head to the face the sun-filled window. "I just — I just wish I could talk with you again," she whispered painfully, with her strained breath hissing like a tea kettle. "Why'd you have to

leave me, too? Why does everyone always end up leaving me?" Alice's throat tightened, choking away any more potential for speech. She looked down at her slippers once more and brought her feet up from the floor and into the bed. Her knees made their way to her chest as she laid herself down onto her side. In no time at all, the pillowcase became a makeshift handkerchief, and the mattress supported her weight safely like her grandmother's lap once had. She rocked back and forth slowly, imagining the rhythm of the old wooden rocking chair until she could hear the wood creaking all around. The creaking turned into thuds.

Knock Knock Knock Knock

Alice jolted upward and out of bed. Her ears rang for a second, and her vision became snowy like the improperly connected television in the living room. She took a brief moment to recover from standing too quickly and grabbed a wad of tissues from her nightstand to wipe her face. She and her furry slippers scurried away anxiously into the living room and then headed toward the front door. When she arrived, she could tell that someone was pacing back and forth across the porch, and she could hear the wood groaning angrily beneath their heavy shoes. She crept toward the window and peeked out of it carefully from behind the dusty blinds.

"What the — is that a cop?" she thought as she opened the curtain a little more to get a better, but much less discreet view of the man. *"What on earth could he want?"* She closed the curtain and wiped her nose and eyes once more onto the sleeve of her nightshirt before reaching for the door handle. As she turned the knob, she inhaled deeply to calm her heart and compose herself a little more. When the door opened, the man stopped pacing and turned to face her.

"Good morning, miss. Sorry to bother you so early, but due to some, uh, recent events, I took it upon myself to give you a little visit." He extended a hand toward Alice. "I'm Detective Blake Darrow from the Wintersburg police station," he continued speaking. "Your name is Alice, correct?"

Alice nodded and returned his handshake. "That's right. Alice Foster. I just moved here yesterday, actually —"

"I know," he interrupted. "That's one of the reasons I came out to see you. We don't get a lot of new people moving into this town, so I wanted to meet with you personally to discuss a few things. Places like this are filled with rumors, and I just thought I'd take it upon myself to give you some facts before the folks tried to scare you off with their nonsense."

"I understand. That's actually really considerate. Would you like to come inside or something? The house is still a mess from all of the moving, but you're welcome to sit and have some coffee." She stepped aside and motioned behind her.

"That'd be nice, thank you," the detective said as he stepped forward. "And don't worry about the mess. I'm sure I've seen much worse."

The pair walked through the living room and into the kitchen. The detective sat down in one of the stools by the counter and fiddled with his badge. Alice walked around to the other side and rummaged through the items that Tiffany had brought over the day before.

"The neighbor gave me a few things yesterday. It looks like the only option for coffee is Colombian roast. Is that okay with you?" she asked, politely. She opened the tin anyway, expecting him to accept the offer.

"Yeah, Colombian is fine. Actually, I'd like to discuss your neighbor first since we're already on the subject." He cleared his throat and ran a hand uncomfortably through his short dark hair.

Alice paused and stared at the

detective anxiously before responding. "Um, she's not a criminal, is she?"

"No, no. It's nothing like that," he said, waving his hands back and forth in the air. "You see, it's just that, well, I'm sure you've noticed the posters of the missing women around town, right?"

"Yeah, I saw one at Medley's yesterday," she replied while scooping the coffee into the filter. She wondered where he was planning on going with the conversation.

"Well, we believe that we might have found one of the women."

Alice gasped. "Really? Are they okay, or..." her voice trailed off as she imagined the possibilities.

Detective Darrow shook his head and looked up at her. "Your neighbor, Tiffany, found a body last night." He cleared his throat. "She had been walking in the woods near the lake and stumbled upon a pretty messed up scene. From the clothing we found, the woman seems to match the description of Jessica Roberts, the first person to have turned up missing in the past few years. We're still waiting on confirmation from her family, but we're pretty sure it's her."

Alice stood still, completely shocked, and then measured out some water from the faucet to pour into the coffee pot. As she poured it in, she tried to think of a proper response, but her mind went wild with all of the possible imagery. The coffee finally dripped and began filling the pot, so she reached for two clean mugs. She moved the pot out of the way and let the coffee stream directly into one of them.

"But," he began again, breaking the silence. "Tiffany, though, she's going to need a friend right now. Since you're her neighbor, I was hoping that you could check on her every now and then. I don't know how well she's going to handle what happened, and her parents don't live nearby from what I've been told. I'm not sure if she really had too many people around to check in with her, at least not in person."

"Yeah, of course. I'll go over and visit her soon. Did she see much, or..."

Detective Darrow nodded and looked down at the counter-top. "She saw more than she needed to see. We took her to the hospital, but they discharged her this morning. I'm pretty sure she'll be okay, but I just think she might need someone to talk to. Someone other than a doctor or a cop."

Alice nodded, filled the second cup, and placed them both down on the counter. "Would you like some creamer?" she asked, trying to maintain an appearance of calmness.

"No, thank you. I'll take it how it is," he replied.

They sipped their hot drinks in silence for a moment. Alice's mind wandered again, taking her through the various possibilities of what could have happened to Jessica. "Was she murdered? Was it an accident? Who could have buried her? Did she die out there, or was she dragged into the woods from somewhere else?" Questions flooded her mind as she stared in the distance at nothing in particular.

"I guess there isn't really much more to discuss," Detective Darrow said, interrupting Alice's thoughts. "I live just down the street if you ever need anything."

"Oh! That's why you looked so familiar. Weren't you walking home from Medley's yesterday, too? I think I saw you behind me."

Detective Darrow's face brightened a bit from her words. "Yeah, that was me. And, sorry about that. I was in a hurry and didn't have the time to properly introduce myself."

Alice let out a small chuckle to try to brighten the mood. "You scared the living daylights out of me, you know. I was just trying to get home and then some strange man came out of nowhere and started running after me. It was terrifying."

Detective Darrow rubbed his eyes as if he were hiding from embarrassment. "I guess I owe you a better apology then. How about this — you can have my personal number. That way, if you feel scared or uncomfortable, but don't think it's a matter for 9-1-1, you can just call me and I can come check on things for you."

A small smile formed on Alice's lips and stayed there while she gathered a pen and scrap piece of paper. "Wow. Such a prize," she said sarcastically, but still amused. "Here, you can use this," she said, sliding the items in front of him.

He picked up the pen and clicked it a few times. "I have my own, but I guess this one's just as good," he stated while writing down his phone number, and only his first name below it.

"Blake," Alice said aloud after she picked up the paper to examine it. "I can call you that? Just Blake? You're sure?"

He nodded and grinned. "Yes, but only when you're calling this number." He pointed directly to the paper in Alice's hand. "If I'm on duty or in uniform, well, you know the drill. Everyone already thinks I'm too relaxed as it is."

"I appreciate it," she said before

turning toward the refrigerator. "I'll keep it there under the magnet. It won't get lost that way."

Detective Darrow stood up and dusted the imaginary dust from his clothes. "I've stayed a bit longer than I meant to, so I should probably get back to the station. Thanks for letting me talk to you in person and for being so hospitable. Even though we all know each other around here, you'd be surprised to hear about how few people would actually invite a cop inside for coffee," he said, with both amusement and uneasiness in his voice. "Anyway, I meant what I said though. If you're ever uncomfortable, just give me a call."

Alice grabbed the mugs and carried them back over to the sink. "Thanks for stopping by, and don't worry. It's nice knowing that there's someone looking out for me, especially now that..." her voice trailed off as she thought of Jessica's photo from the poster.

Detective Darrow looked at her knowingly. "We don't know what or who we're dealing with out there. Just keep your doors and windows locked, and try to let someone know what you're doing and where you'll be if you decide to go out somewhere." He stood up, walked toward the living room, and paused by the front door. "Oh, and one more thing," he began again. "You're working at Edna's now, right?"

"Wow, you just know everything, huh?" Alice said, surprised. "Yeah, she agreed to give me a booth. Why? What's up?"

"If you wouldn't mind, could I stop by some time? I'll be due for a haircut soon. Gotta stay sharp."

"Come by whenever," Alice replied, rolling her eyes to disguise her amusement. "Now get out of here. Don't you have a bad guy to catch or something?"

Detective Darrow smiled and walked out the door, pausing briefly to turn around and look at Alice one more time before continuing on toward his car.

Alice waved and shut the door behind him. *"What a strange man."* she thought. *"These small-town cops get really personal."*

Her friendly mask faded, and worry appeared across her face once more in its place.

***

That evening after work, Alice got out of her car and walked over to Tiffany's porch instead of her own. With Detective Darrow's request still on her mind, she figured that it would probably be best to check on her neighbor sooner, rather than later. She approached the door and knocked gently, hoping that she wouldn't startle her too much. For extra reassurance, she decided to announce her identity.

"Tiffany? It's me, Alice, from next door." She paused, wondering if she was being more intrusive than helpful.

The doorknob rattled for a second before it turned completely, and Tiffany's face appeared in front of her. "Alice. Thank God it's just you," she said, exasperated. "I'm guessing you've already heard what happened."

"I haven't heard much, but I wanted to check on you. I don't think the news has spread too far. Even the ladies over at Edna's weren't talking about it yet. From my understanding, that's where news usually travels first."

Tiffany grinned. "You're not wrong, I guess. Here, come in."

Alice followed her inside and into the living room. At first glance, the house seemed to have a very similar layout to her own, but it was far more decorated. Paintings and other artwork covered the beige walls, and ceramic knickknacks occupied most of the space on her tables and counter-tops. The air was filled with the fragrances of several differing candles, making the combined scent unidentifiable and completely unique. She sat down on the small worn couch and watched as Tiffany headed toward the kitchen.

"Help yourself to the remote. I'll grab us a few drinks. You like beer, right?" Tiffany called out as she walked toward the refrigerator.

"Beer's fine. Oh, um, hey, Tiffany?"

"Yeah, what's up?" she asked as she returned with two frosty cans in her grip.

Alice reached out to accept one and quickly cracked it open. "Do you think the others will turn up?" she asked before taking a small sip. "I mean, do you think they could be buried somewhere around here too?"

Tiffany stood frozen for a moment. "I — Wow. You really just jump right into the good questions, huh?"

Alice put her hand over her mouth dramatically before attempting to explain herself. "Shit. I didn't mean to. It's just, this has been on my mind all day. I'm really sorry... honestly."

Tiffany shook her head and replied. "No, it's okay. I understand. I've been thinking about the other girls too. I was able to listen in on some of the conversations at the station, and I heard that the cops did a quick search of the area, but didn't find anything else. Who knows what could have happened, really..."

Alice took a few deep gulps from her beer. "You're doing okay, though, right?" she asked, feeling rude for her lack of tact.

Tiffany nodded. "It was terrifying — I won't lie, but to be honest, I feel more numb now than anything." She took a long swig and blew a muted burp to the side. "It's weird. It feels like a dream, I guess. Maybe it just hasn't really hit me yet."

Alice finished her beer after a few more gulps and sat the empty can down on the coffee table. "I know that we don't really know each other yet, but I do know what it's like to have to go through things on your own, and hard it can be to open up to someone. Just know that my door's always open to you, no matter what time it is, or what you need. You can always stop by."

Tiffany looked up from the table to meet Alice's eyes. "You're a lot like her, ya know."

"Like who?" Alice asked with a confused expression.

"Sarah," she answered softly as if the name was a secret. She began picking nervously at her fingernails and continued her thought process. "She had a big heart. I don't know of one person who didn't enjoy being around her. She really was magnetic. Wherever we would go, people would stop what they were doing to see how she was or what her plans were later. She was probably the only reason I even had friends." Tiffany stopped speaking for a moment to wipe her eyes. "I'm sorry. Maybe I'm a little sensitive after all."

Alice scooted closer to pat Tiffany gently and comfortingly on her back. "I understand. You don't need to apologize for anything. This is a lot for anyone to handle, and you've lost a friend on top of it all. You'd have to be as cold as ice to not react in some way."

"Thanks, it's just that —" Tiffany began again, "I really miss her, and when I fell... in the woods..." Her voice became tighter and strained as she continued. "... For a second, I thought that it was her. This is going to sound crazy, but I was almost relieved when I thought it was Sarah's body."

Alice looked up at her, startled, and stopped patting her on the back. She froze as if she'd just seen a ghost, and was suddenly very concerned with the direction the conversation was taking. Her face was unable to mask her uncomfortable expression or her startled eyes.

"Dammit. Don't look at me like that,"

Tiffany said defensively as she brushed Alice's heavy hand from her shoulder. "I know what you're thinking and that's not what I meant. I'd never wish harm on her. She was my best friend." She wiped her eyes once more and stood up from the couch. "Sorry again, I didn't mean to get upset like that," she stated as she walked back toward the kitchen for more beer. "It's just really hard not knowing what happened. I think it's even harder than finding the dead body to be completely honest. Sarah's been gone for almost two months now and no one has any leads or answers. I feel like I'm going crazy just waiting around."

Alice nodded. "I think I know what you mean. I just lost my grandmother before moving here, and the circumstances surrounding her death were, well, not exactly normal. I'd do almost anything for answers, including moving to a small town where I don't know anyone, apparently."

"Really? How'd she pass?" Tiffany asked.

"It was a train," she said. "The cops told me that she had been out on the tracks late at night and wouldn't move no matter how many times the horn was sounded. The engineer told them that she didn't even look back once." Alice coughed lightly and looked down at her feet. "She just kept walking. They called it an accident, but I really don't see how. Her sight and hearing were fine. She wasn't in perfect health, but she definitely could have moved out of the way. I don't even know why she was out there. She hated trains."

"Goodness, I'm so sorry. Did she talk to anyone before she went, or had she been acting differently?" Tiffany asked, suddenly very interested.

Alice looked up. "She hadn't talked to anyone that I know of, and she seemed fine that morning, too. That's the reason I'm here though. She grew up in Wintersburg, and I feel like even though I'll probably never know what really happened, I can be a little closer to her here."

Tiffany nodded. "Thanks for sharing that with me. I guess we have even more in common than I thought."

"There's always company in pain," Alice replied, looking up with a partial smile.

"I can drink to that!" Tiffany said, holding a beer in the air.

Alice grabbed another one off of the table, popped the tab, and raised the can as well.

"Cheers, if we can even call it that."

"Cheers."

Chapter 4

"Three's Company"

The salon seemed different the following day. There were women under every dryer and in every styling chair, including Alice's. It was as if the blow dryers were mimicking the static-laced sounds of a television, and the hair foils were the closest thing to an antenna in the area. Everyone tuned in to hear the news, share the news, and make up their own news related to the body that had been found near the lake. Alice had finally begun to truly understand the warnings that she had been receiving about the amount of gossip that plagued the town. She was a hairdresser, after all, so she definitely was no stranger to juicy stories, ranging from marital troubles to election scandals, but Wintersburg had its own unique style. While many things were fact-checked, corrected, or just blatantly dismissed by her previous clientele, no one in this town listened to anything unless it was flavored with exciting misinformation.

"That's what she gets for being drunk all the time. I haven't seen her sober since she was a kid in Sunday school," a plump elderly woman said as she slightly raised the hood of her dryer. "I bet she ran off with the first person to offer her a bed and a bottle." The woman nodded, agreeing with herself. "She probably tried to steal from someone and got what she deserved instead."

A frail woman in the seat next to her lifted an index finger up to her lips and shook her head in protest. "Eleanor, we all know she was a lush, but that doesn't mean she deserved to be left out in a shallow grave somewhere. Goodness gracious," she stated, scolding the woman like a child. "Let's not pretend like your son doesn't do his fair share of drinking, also."

"My son is a good man. He's not some bar-hopping wretch like Jessica. For Pete's sake, she was almost 30 and never worked a day in her life, unless you count those nights she spent lying on her back for every trucker who passed through here."

"Daniel might be a good man, but I heard that he thought Jess was pretty good, too," a slightly younger woman chimed in from the waiting area. "I saw them making out last year at Kirt's Pub. If you ask me, I think he would have laid on his back for her."

A few women struggled to keep their amusement and giggles hidden.

"What do you know, June?" Eleanor replied sarcastically to the woman, clearly offended and ashamed. "I'm surprised you can even see anything with those hideous bangs in your eyes anyway."

"Yeah, yeah. Keep on talking. Get your cardio for the day by runnin' your mouth, grandma. Girls keep going missing, and you could be added to that list at any moment if anyone was able to lift your ass off of the couch."

Eleanor sighed defeatedly and shifted her weight in the chair.

The frail woman made eye contact

with June and shook her head gently. She quickly tilted her chin upward and gestured toward a dark-haired woman who sat motionlessly, receiving a perm from a very visibly uncomfortable stylist.

The salon went cold and silent for a moment until the muffled sounds of crying made themselves more noticeable. The dark-haired woman, about fifty years old, had gotten up to grab a tissue from the front desk. She stood there, still, like a small and withered tree, wiping the dew from her eyes.

"Betty, they'll find Sarah. She wasn't wild like the others," Edna said while combing through the curls of one of her clients. "The other three were known for getting into trouble. Sarah was a good girl. She probably just wanted to get out and see the world. You know how the young ones are these days. There's not much of a future for them in a place like this."

Betty sobbed louder and darted toward the exit, with rollers still pinned in her hair.

"What was that about?" Alice asked, looking around the room in surprise.

"That's one of the missing girl's moms," Eleanor stated. "The fourth girl, Sarah. Actually, didn't you just move into her old house?"

"Geez, you know everyone's business,

don't you?" June piped up from the waiting area.

"Edna, can you comb her hair out?" Alice asked, pointing to the woman in her styling chair as she ran outside, chasing after Betty.

Before Edna could properly respond, Alice ran out the door in an attempt to catch up to Betty before she could drive away. She saw a glimpse of her across the parking lot and caught up just as she had hopped inside and closed the door. Alice tapped gently on the glass window.

"Betty? I know you don't know me, but you seem like you need someone to talk to right now," she said, while internally questioning why she even had such a strong urge to follow this woman.

Betty leaned forward and rolled her window down while Alice continued speaking.

"My name's Alice. I didn't know your daughter, but —" She tried to come up with a reasonable explanation.

Betty pointed to the seat beside her and unlocked the passenger's side door. She grabbed a pack of cigarettes from the purse in her lap and lit one with the lighter that shook softly in her weak hand. The woman's cropped black hair was partially set into orange plastic rollers which had become loose from the wind. Between the smoke that escaped from her mouth and nose, and the combination of colors, she looked like Halloween, but not in a frightening way. She was more like a pale jack-o'-lantern who had just happened to light her own flame. Though, she did appear to have been dramatically withered from a season's change. It was as if she had been left on the porch to dry out and become nature's responsibility to clean up and do away with.

Alice made her way over to the door and let herself inside. The car smelled like fire and old vanilla candles — the ones that could often be found stored away in a forgotten closet with a thick layer of dust caked to the wick. Once she plopped down, her pantyhose snagged against a piece of torn faux-leather that had been protruding defiantly from the seat. She moved her hand downward, and applied pressure to the runner, hoping that she could stop it from traveling any more.

"Oh, darn it. I've got a run in my hose again," Alice said with a hushed and frustrated voice.

Betty shifted in her seat and reached behind her to the floor. She retrieved a small black purse and began to dig through its contents. "Here. Use this," she said as she lifted a clear bottle of nail polish in the air.

"Paint it across the whole thing, and it'll keep it from getting bigger."

Alice grabbed the glass bottle and smiled slightly. She twirled it in between her fingertips while appreciating the way that it reflected the light like a polished crystal. Her grandmother's once-sparkling eyes came into her mind, and she stopped moving it around. "You know, my grandma always used nail polish for these type of things too. She never thought to buy a clear one though, so she always had a few bright-colored splotches all over her legs." She let out a little laugh. "I remember always thinking that the holes would have looked less obvious than the polish, even as a little girl."

Betty gave her a small smile and continued to blow smoke all around the car. Her chest raised and lowered at a steadier speed than before, and it became apparent that she was finally calming down. The puffy bags under her eyes seemed to be bruised and swollen, probably from a lack of sleep and an abundance of tears. They were the evidence of the type of mourning that only a parent could be capable of knowing — the type of emptiness that could cause a heart to fail or a mind to shatter.

"I used to paint Sarah's nails every Saturday," Betty began. "When she was little, I mean. I used to take her down to the lake in the mornings, and we'd skip stones until our hands were absolutely filthy." She paused for a second to stare at her veiny thrombosed hands and a hot tear trailed down her chin and neck. She wiped it away and pursed her lips into a shape that almost resembled a heart. "I'd tell her that we had no choice but to get manicures afterward, that we had to look pretty in case there were any handsome princes around. I'd pull out the same red polish from my pocket and hide it under a few stones when she would look away. Sarah! I'd call to her. Sarah, look what I've found! and then I'd dig it out of the rubble, hinting that a fairy must have left it for us. She'd always act so surprised, but I knew that she was just playing along. We'd rinse our hands in the lake water and sit together on one of the large flat rocks. Then, she'd give me one of her little hands, and I'd paint each nail while telling her stories about frogs, princesses, and castles..."

Betty's smile became more and more toothy until it was obvious that she hadn't been smiling at all. A long animal-like whine escaped from the space between her teeth — a single unwavering note that could send chills down the spine of the devil, himself. If pain had a sound, surely this was it. When it came time for her to inhale, she snorted and snotted while wiping away at her own face. Her heart sang its song once more, and she buried her hands into her hairline.

Alice gasped and pulled her in for a long hug, or as much of a hug as she could manage with the car's center console in the way. She pat Betty's shoulder, working as a metronome for her whine.

Thump Thump Thump Thump

Alice felt her mind wandering back in time. She envisioned Grandma Susan holding her on her lap, rocking her, telling her that everything would be okay. This was a scene that she escaped to often, mostly when she needed comforting of her own though. Perhaps she wasn't trying to calm Betty as much as she was trying to calm herself.

Betty broke away gently from the embrace and wiped the rest of the depressing goo off of her face. She reached for another cigarette and lit it with a more confident hand than before. As she exhaled storm-clouds into the dashboard, she stared ahead, seemingly at nothing in particular. She appeared as if her mind had completely left the world.

Alice reached over to Betty's hair and began to unpin the rollers, letting a few small curls bounce away from her grip, defying gravity. Each one sprung around like a metal slinky, toppling over one another clumsily. The short ringlets glistened from an over-use of mousse and contrasted greatly with the rest of her straight fine hair. "If you'd like to come back in, I can redo these for you. I don't think the ladies will say anything else today."

Betty shook her head and looked down at her lap. "No, not today. I'll try to come back later in the week. Actually, I should really be going."

Alice nodded. "I understand. Well, I'm here most days. If you ever want to talk —" she stopped herself abruptly after feeling a shift in the air.

Betty tossed her still-lit cigarette out of the window and grabbed Alice's hand with the both of hers. She held it there, gripping it tightly as she stared into her eyes. Sanity seemed to have left her skull as if it had leaked out of her tear-ducts during the crying fit. She leaned in closer to Alice, squeezing her bones even tighter when she felt a slight resistance. She pulled her arm toward her chest and then gripped Alice's wrist with a surprisingly strong fist as she feathered her fingertips across her acrylic nails. A few fresh tears fell from Betty's eyes onto Alice's cuticles, followed by a long stream of mucous that had escaped from her nose.

"Your hands are all dirty, Sarah," Betty

said in a sickly-sweet baby voice. "Let's get them cleaned up. We wouldn't want to scare any handsome princes away, would we?"

Alice wanted to jump back, to scream, to smack — anything, but she was frozen from disbelief. Her muscles relaxed, and she was unable to find the strength pull away anymore.

"Come on. Let's paint your nails again, sweetheart." Betty grabbed the clear polish that had been resting in Alice's lap and unscrewed it with her molars. She sat the open bottle down on the console and began brushing it all across Alice's fingers, not even bothering to acknowledge where her nails were located anymore. "I've missed you so much, Sarah."

***

Alice walked somberly to the bathroom and turned on the shower to wash the day away. The faucet let out a long squeak, and the sound of Betty's wailing raped her ears once more. She shook the memory from her mind and stepped beneath the hot stream of water. She scrubbed at her arms and hands, peeling away little plastic-like pieces of polish that had coated her fingers like a toxic pastry glaze. The fragments glittered and reflected light back toward her before they finally met their demise in the drain. She stomped her feet over the metal to assure herself that they wouldn't be coming back.

After she was finished, she wiped herself off with a towel, put on some clean pajamas, and started to dry her hair with the blow dryer back in the bathroom. The steam finally dissipated from the mirror, and she was able to see her reflection more clearly. She stared at herself, expressionless, while she brushed through her shoulder-length hair. She didn't bother styling it or fluffing up her bangs like she usually would in the mornings. She just wanted it to be dry and finished.

Unfortunately, the house was older, so the electric wasn't very reliable or predictable. That particular bathroom outlet couldn't handle the blow dryer being on a hot setting, and it caused the breaker to trip. Alice jumped from the sudden silent darkness but quickly realized what had happened. With damp hair, she made her way down to the basement and found the breaker box. She flipped the switch and heard the blow dryer kick back on upstairs.

"Ugh. I should have turned that off before I came down here," she thought, annoyed with herself. She turned around quickly to dart back up the stairs but noticed a cardboard box in the far corner of the room under the laundry folding table. She crept over to the box and lifted the lid. It was

covered in cobwebs and appeared to have just been shoved under the table and forgotten about for at least a year, or even more. As she examined the contents on top, she discovered a few photos stacked together and started to go through them. By the second picture, it became very obvious that she was looking through Sarah's belongings. Alice stared at the girl in the photo, realizing that Sarah was probably the last person to have touched the contents of this box. Her features were a lot more clear in these particular photos than they had been in the blurry black-and-white photocopied flyer at Medley's. An uncomfortable mixture of clarity and anxiety filled her body as Sarah's face smiled up at her from the glossy paper.

"Whoa... we really do look alike..."

Chapter 5

"Total Eclipse of the Heart"

The sky was darker than usual that evening. Anyone who looked up for too long, whether searching for the moon or for the stars, was pulled into its depths. It was as if the sky was some kind of a black hole. It wanted company badly as it hovered above

Wintersburg, looking for lonely eyes.

Betty glanced up from her canvas and stared out the window, taking notice of the uncomfortable lack of moonlight. Usually, she would be able to paint while watching an array of sparkling reflections dance across the lake, but tonight there was only blackness. The lake might as well have been a giant lump of coal. Unenthusiastically, she reached across the table to a small antiquated lamp and turned it on before resting her paintbrush inside one of the plastic cups in front of her. She picked up a matching cup and poured herself another generous helping of cheap wine. Her feet kicked at an empty bottle that sat sideways on the floor. While she had every intention of finishing this second bottle as well, she was too set in her ways to sip straight from its narrow neck. From paint to alcohol, pouring was what she did best.

She turned back to her canvas, mixed a shade of red, and added a few brush strokes here and there. She carefully outlined and then filled Sarah's lips before dipping her brush back into the water cup to rinse it off. The water swirled around and then turned crimson from the concentrated pigment. She set her brush on a paper towel and glanced at her palette, unsure of what to do next. The drinks had really started to kick in, and their poison was starting to hinder her talents.

Betty sighed heavily and reached for her cup of wine once more. She took a long and loving gulp as she sat there resembling an open-mouthed baby bird. She hadn't been much of a drinker in her previous years, but alcohol had recently become as necessary as oxygen for her to go about her days.

A second gulp went down her gullet.

And one more.

On the fourth gulp, her nostrils awakened and her taste buds sensed that something was wrong.

"Paint."

She gagged and choked several times before she involuntarily produced a bright red liquid from her throat. She tried to hold it in, and even made an admirable attempt to cover her mouth, but she failed. The colored water sprayed out from between her fingers like hot lava. It tainted everything within five feet of her with what could easily be compared to blood droplets.

She retched again and realized that she'd confused the two cups.

Her body felt hot and heavy as the contents of her belly danced up the crevices of her esophagus, tangoing around potential ulcers. An angry froth began to swing from her dangling uvula before it finally made a grand entrance into the world. The paint and water twirled together and her head felt as if it were spinning along to the same gurgling song. The contractions led, and Betty followed. More spasms encouraged her to buckle over, so she dipped, and her head snapped toward the canvas. In one huge finale, one beautiful ending to an unconventional performance, Betty's mouth sprayed everything like a rusty garden sprinkler. She splattered Sarah's image with a glorious polka-dotted pattern that resembled one of her favorite dresses.

Betty's lively eyes met Sarah's empty gaze, and she sobbed. She reached toward the canvas and started smearing the paint all around beneath the weight of her palms.

"Stop bleeding! I have to stop the bleeding!" She yelped like an injured dog and her mind briefly wandered back to the time that she had hit a beagle with her car. She had been driving Sarah to a sleepover one evening, a decade prior, and was still unable to forgive herself for the accident. The cries haunted Betty each time she saw a dog, no matter how happy or healthy it was. She couldn't forget the way that it had looked up at her from the wet blacktop, the way that it had cried out to her, begging her — the one whose distracted mind had caused its pain — for help. It seemed only fitting that she was now the one crying from the ground, covered in crimson.

The neighbor's mutt howled in the distance at the moonless sky, and Betty's yelping turned into long chilling moans of the same key and volume. She sang along with it for quite some time as she continued to wipe away futilely at the canvas. The penciled sketch smudged around, infecting the paint with charcoal, and Sarah's face muddied under Betty's paws.

Betty became rabid.

She lifted herself from the ground and pushed both hands into the slippery table to steady her weight. She stood there with a curved spine as she supported herself with locked elbows. Drool dripped from her lips, still slightly blemished from the paint, and she stared blankly at the cup of wine.

She lifted the cup and drank, taking a moment to fully acknowledge the flavors of only the first gulp before she burped everything back out onto the wet floor. Her stomach was too irritated to take in any more fluids, but she was too drunk to realize the problem. She tried once more to fill herself with the wine but gagged before even a drop was able to touch her tongue. She slammed the cup back onto the table, crinkling the plastic from the tightness of her grip, and picked up the glass bottle.

Betty raised it in the air like a drunken pirate and stumbled backward a few paces while still managing to stay on her feet. She began to mock and scold the family portraits that were hanging from the walls, calling out almost-comical obscenities between belches and hiccups.

"Roger, you fat piece of shit!"

Hic

"You fat Big Bird piece of shit!" She turned to face the opposite wall. "And you!" she snarled, pointing at a black-and-white photograph of an elderly woman. "You said that everything would be okay. You lied to my face!"

Betty tossed the wine bottle at the photo, and missed, of course. A few large sharp chunks broke off, but overall it maintained most of its recognizable shape. She stumbled forward and leaned back into the table. As she looked downward, she chuckled quietly. More stretchy drool escaped from her sour mouth, re-wetting the foamy corners of her lips. "She's not gone," she said flatly. "She just isn't feeling well. I should take some soup over to her house."

Betty wobbled toward the kitchen and fumbled with one of the knobs on the gas stove. It clicked at her several times but produced no flame. While smacking her lips back at it mockingly, she turned the knob a few more times, but still had no success. She fumbled around in a drawer nearby, and eventually found a long lighter. She held it near the burner and clicked it one more time. As soon as she heard the sound, a bright and agitated flame erupted into a blazing lion's mane but quickly settled itself back down into a blueish ring. She stared into it as if it were a singular eye staring back at her.

She placed a warped and discolored pot onto the burner and feverishly cranked away at a tin can of store-bought chicken soup. Each crank of the can opener was an obvious struggle for her disobedient joints and muscles, but she persevered until she had created enough of a space for the soup to escape. She bent the lid back, and just barely missed slicing her finger open. The metal grazed softly across her skin as if it was warning her to be more careful next time, but it caused no wounds.

Betty poured the soup and some sink water into the pot and then stirred it all together until it was a fragrant yellowish mixture. She dropped the empty can on the floor but was too focused on maintaining her balance to retrieve it. She continued to stir for a few seconds until deciding that the soup was probably warm enough. It wasn't, but that's not what mattered.

She poured it into a marinara-stained plastic container, attached a lid, and sat it on the counter while she retrieved her jacket. "Sarah will love this," she mumbled, still smiling through partially-crystallized snot and tears. "She will absolutely love it."

***

Alice sat in her living room, watching the TV at a lower than reasonable volume. She wasn't really paying attention to any of the shows' plots as much as she was just leaving everything on to maintain a sense of companionship while she winded down from the workday (and while trying to forget the uncomfortable encounter with Betty). Hearing the actors' cheerful voices and seeing their excited faces provided a sense of calmness and company for her. She didn't need to know why the characters were happy or what they were doing. She was perfectly content to know that they were just there, nearby, and almost tangible.

She stood up to fetch another slice of pizza from the kitchen after she had reminded herself that the food would be getting cold soon. Cold pizza was great for a quick breakfast, but definitely not for nights spent alone. She opened the delivery box again and scooped a fresh warm piece onto her already-greasy paper plate, and then took the remaining slices over to the refrigerator.

"I guess it's a good thing I didn't buy

too many groceries yet," she thought. *"I can fit the whole box in here for tomorrow."* Her mind wandered to the dried slices that Sarah had left behind, and she soon found herself wondering what other things might have been lingering around the house, or even in that cardboard box she'd found in the basement earlier. As she imagined little trinkets and hidden diaries, she leaned against the counter and took a very generous bite of her slice. The sauce and cheese were like heaven to her taste buds, and her tongue was awakened even more by the fizzy cola that she chugged to wash it all down. Kirt's Pub might have been a little trashy, but the staff certainly made good food. She made a mental note of that.

Her thoughts were interrupted by the sound of footsteps near the backdoor. There was an uneven stone path that led from the sidewalk up to the kitchen. It was littered with stray pieces of gravel and rock that would grind loudly under the shoes of anyone who used it. Alice stayed still, almost forgetting to breathe, as she listened to the crunching sounds. Whoever it was, was trying to stay quiet, because their steps were slow and deliberate. They knew to avoid stepping off of the path. The grass was patchy, and the ground was deceptively soft. Even the weight of a squirrel could leave a print in the mud that surrounded the stones. This was a person who knew the property and didn't want to leave a trace. There was silence for a handful of seconds — seconds that felt like minutes. Every muscle in Alice's body tensed, and her ears began to ring from the nervous increase in blood pressure.

The door handle turned.

Crash!

Alice jumped up and bumped her elbow on the edge of the counter-top. She grabbed her arm instinctively and turned her head to face the noise. Someone was outside of the front door now but was being a lot less careful than whoever had crept up to the kitchen.

Behind her, she heard the trashcans by the stone pathway fall over, and the large crunching steps of someone running away. Adrenaline finally kicked in, and she quickly locked the back door in case that person decided to return later. She grabbed a chopping knife from a drawer and ran into the living room. Her index finger pulled slightly at the blinds, creating a space just large enough to see through. Alice gripped the handle tightly and leaned in to take a look.

"Betty?"

Confusion filled her mind as she loosened her grip and fumbled with the door's deadbolt. She opened it quickly, and dropped the knife to the ground, just barely missing one of her naked feet. The concrete porch felt like ice beneath her soles, contrasting with the heat that radiated from her cheeks.

"Betty! Betty!" She shook Betty's heavy body, trying to wake her. A few gurgles and exhausted moans slipped out from her mouth, but nothing more than that. "Betty! Can you hear me?" she yelled, with a cracking voice. "Wake up! Betty!"

Alice lightly smacked at her face and pinched her cheeks, but there was still no response. She ran back inside and into the kitchen. In what seemed like one sweeping motion, she grabbed the phone, un-twirled the tangled coffee-stained cord, and called the cops.

"9 1 1, what's your emergency"

"There — there's a woman on my porch. She fell, I think. I — I can't wake her, but she's still breathing."

"What's your location, miss?"

"472 Fifth street, in Wintersburg. Please hurry."

"Okay, Miss, if you could stay on the line —"

Click.

In a matter of minutes, sirens filled the air, and the ambulance's lights illuminated the front porch. Alice sat on the concrete with Betty's head propped up on her lap. The lights allowed her to see a little better, and she noticed a mess of paint and other stains all over Betty's face and clothing. A few feet away, there was a spilled container of some sort.

"What in the world is that?" she wondered while examining the barely-breathing woman.

A patrol car arrived just as the medics were wheeling a gurney to the porch. The medics carefully lifted Betty, strapped her down securely, and pushed her back to their vehicle. Detective Darrow cut his engine, shut his car door, and gave the medics a little nod of gratitude.

"What happened here tonight, Miss Foster?" he asked while approaching, seeming a lot more formal than he had during their first encounter.

"I don't know, honestly. I was in my kitchen, and I heard someone out back. Then there was a big crash on the front porch... and there she was, just lying here."

"Did you talk to her at all? Do you know this woman or why she might have come out here?"

"Her name is Betty. She gets her hair done at Edna's salon, but I don't know her last n —"

"Noe. Betty Noe," he said, in a matter-of-fact tone. "You might have seen one of her flyers hanging up outside of Medley's. She's also your landlord Roger's sister."

"She is? I knew she was Sarah's mom — is Sarah's mom, I mean, but I didn't know that she was related to Roger too."

"Small world, huh?" he asked. "It seems like everyone is related in some way around here."

"It really does. What are the flyers for anyway? Does she run a business or something?"

"She sells pulled pork — the good stuff. Now that it's getting warmer out, she should be back to smoking ribs and brisket again too." Detective Darrow shifted his weight and stepped up onto the porch. He held a little notepad and a pen that seemed tiny in his large hands. He pointed to a visibly wet spot on the porch with the pen's tip. "So, that's where she was?"

"Yeah, she tripped, I think. Oh, and she brought that container with her."

He nodded.

"Blake — I mean, uh, Detective. She doesn't have a key, does she? To the house, I mean?"

"I saw Roger changing these locks about a week before you moved in. She has no reason to have one anymore."

Alice sighed with relief and unfolded her arms from across her chest. "That's good, at least."

"Don't worry about it too much, Miss Foster. Betty's been a little weird since Sarah went missing, but she's pretty harmless. She just has a lot on her plate right now, between the stress of Sarah, and having to take care of Will."

"Will? Is that her son?"

Detective Darrow shook his head. "It's her younger brother. You've got Roger, Betty, and Will. Their mom, Judy, used to take care of him, but cancer took her a few years ago, and the responsibility fell on Betty."

"Oh, so he's sick, or..."

"Not sick, he's just not alright to live alone. I'm sure you'll see him around. He spends most of his days walking through the town or hanging around Medley's." He turned and looked back at his patrol car. "Anyway, I've got to get out of here. There's a lot going on at the station tonight, and I have to follow up with this at the hospital or the chief will have my throat."

"Yeah, I understand."

"Stay safe." He lowered his chin, and then hurried to his car.

"Oh, Detective!" she called toward him from the doorway. "What about the noises I heard around back? I could have sworn someone was trying to get in."

"Keep your doors locked for now. We didn't see anyone around the house, but I'll stop by in the morning to check it out again."

Alice nodded and shut the door behind herself.

Chapter 6
"Scarface"

The town and its people were feeling a lot friendlier as Alice grew more familiar with her place in the salon. The chairs were filled with large personalities — some cheerful, some miserable, but she noticed that they all joined perfectly together like pieces of a really strange puzzle. Perhaps she actually fit in with these small-town folk more than she'd ever fit in with the city slickers of Parkington. Her clothes might have been a little flashy at times, but she loved the quiet simplicity of Wintersburg, with its single family-owned grocery store that fed the entire town, the lack of traffic lights or smog while driving, and the tiny salon where all of the women congregated like loud geese waiting to have their feathers groomed. This was it. This was where she was meant to be all along.

She never really had much in common with any of the girls in the city. Sure, she wore the latest fashions and had a few friends while growing up, but she never really had a best friend or a clique to belong to. When she graduated and went on to beauty school, she would occasionally meet up with a few of the girls after classes for food or drinks, but the invitations stopped once the certificates were handed out. Alice was used to being alone, but she didn't exactly like it. She hid her insecurities behind teased hair and long lashes, and she faked enough confidence to get through the days unscathed.

In Wintersburg, though, she didn't feel the need to fake anything. The pace was slower, and each time she inhaled the clean air, she felt like she was finally home. Her boss, Edna, had become something like a motherly presence in her life, too. She was constantly checking in with Alice, making sure that she was adjusting well to everything. She would even stop by her house with baked goods, random kitchen utensils that she had found on sale, and decorations that she claimed to have had lying around already. Conveniently, they all seemed to match the ones that Alice had brought along with her from Parkington.

She knew that Edna had been going out of her way to buy these things for her, but she played along with her stories anyway. Each time she heard the doorbell ring, she'd smile and accept the newest thing that Edna would swear to have just stumbled upon the night before while cleaning. Even though she was typically opposed to anything that resembled a hand-out, Alice knew the importance of accepting those little odds and ends. Edna's daughter had started a life of her own several states away and was no longer in her mother's life. Alice held her hands and arms open, knowing that she was filling a void in her life. She didn't have to play the role, but she knew how cold and lonely voids like that could be.

***

The bell that Edna had tied to the front door rang out across the salon and all eyes turned toward the entrance. Alice wondered what everyone was looking at, considering the fact that people had been coming and going all day long, and no one had paid any attention to the chiming sounds before. She turned her head to see what could have been so interesting this time and allowed her hands to pin a roller into her client's hair, using only her muscle memory.

"Hey, Benji! How is everything today?" Edna's voice called out as she walked toward the entrance.

A few elderly women giggled to each other and stared at the man, admiring his good looks. They whispered back and forth between ears that were partially blocked by perm rods and bounced their arthritic knees with excitement. It was as if they were staring at someone with the well-groomed looks of Clark Gable, and the alluring danger and adventure of John Wayne.

"Hey there, Edna," the young man said with a deep, but calming tone. "Just here to do the usual." He sat a black canvas bag on the front desk and plopped himself into the receptionist's seat with an air of confidence. He wore blue jeans and a white t-shirt. His light brown hair was neatly cropped, but still somehow messy as if he'd been driving with the windows rolled down all day. He was definitely easy on the eyes, and his calm, relaxed presence just made the women fawn over him even more. Compared to their low opinions of their husbands, he was like a perfectly frosted cake — one that could be devoured endlessly without causing a single ounce of weight gain.

Alice had seen plenty of handsome men before, so she wasn't entirely impressed. She definitely found him to be more attractive than a lot of the guys around town, though. Her eyes met his, and she turned around to roll the rest of her client's hair. She wasn't going to be distracted by him. There were better things to focus on, like earning money.

Benji started to talk quietly with Edna, and Alice glanced back every so often through the reflection in the mirror. After a short while, she saw Benji raise his hand and point in her direction.

"Susie's girl! Come here! I have someone for you to meet," Edna said, waving her over.

Alice placed her utensils down and excused herself. The sleepy client in her chair nodded and pulled a book from her bag. She didn't seem upset with the interruption.

"Hi there," she said, extending a hand out to Benji. "I'm Alice."

He grabbed her hand and shook it firmly. "Oh, it's so sticky," he said, grinning.

She pulled her hand back and wiped it onto her blouse. "Yikes, yeah, sorry about that. I have mousse all over me right now."

"I'm just kidding with you. I'm Benji. Edna says that you just moved here...?" He looked around the room, pretending that he was only partially interested.

"Oh — yeah, she was nice enough to give me a job here."

"That's great," he replied. "I stop by this place every week. If you ever need your shears sharpened, I'm your guy." He spoke to her with confidence, as if she was an old friend of his and they had simply been getting reacquainted with each other.

"Benji works at Pete's barbershop over by Medley's," Edna added in quickly. "He runs errands for us, and he's really good at sharpening, too. His prices are modest."

"The first time is free, too," he said with a smirk on his face.

"My shears are pretty good right now, but I'll let you know when they could use some help."

Alice noticed an interesting texture on Benji's skin. It looked as if he had tried to cover long thin scars on his cheek and jawline with a thick layer of makeup. She wondered what could have caused such injuries. The markings, from what she could see, were close together and looked almost like someone had dragged their sharp fingernails across his face. He could have been involved in some sort of blade-related accident, though, considering he sharpened things for side cash. Either way, she decided that it was best to avoid staring for too long. There was a big difference between being curious and being rude.

"That sounds like a plan then," he said, cheerfully. "And speaking of plans, since you're new to this area, I could show you around sometime. It might seem like a dull little place, but this town has a lot of interesting things if you know where to look."

"I don't know about all that," she replied. "I think I've already seen just about everything already."

"I promise you haven't. Here, let me give you my number in case you change your mind." He walked over to one of the stylist's stations and grabbed a piece of perming paper from a small beige box. Seven digits scribbled out onto the paper from a partially-dried pen. "There you go. Feel free to leave me something on the machine if I don't pick up. I'm always out doing different things, so I end up missing most of my phone calls."

Alice grabbed the perm paper and placed it into her pocket without even glancing at it. "It was nice to meet you. I really have to get back to Mary though. She'll fall asleep if I leave her alone for much longer."

"I understand. It was nice to meet you, Alice." He smirked, and chills ran down her spine.

Alice wasn't sure what was so off-putting about the guy, but she usually trusted her instincts with people. He seemed nice, likable by everyone, handsome, and hard-working, so what was this awful feeling in her gut? She actively decided not to dwell on it and blamed it on having not been around a flirty male in quite a while.

***

Alice fumbled with her keys as she stood in front of her door. The wind pushed through her hair, causing a few strands to float into her face, making the task even more difficult. She sat a gallon of milk down beside her feet, along with two grocery bags, and finally managed to get the key into the lock. She turned it, picked everything back up, and let herself inside, exhausted from the day.

Grunting lightly with fatigue, she heaved the bags onto the kitchen counter and quickly shoved the milk into the fridge. She leaned against the cold door and her back slid down slowly, while she ran both of her hands through the hair by her temples. Her knees folded up to her chest as she reached the floor. She sat there for a while until the rattling of another pair of keys broke through the silence. Alice raised her head and saw the back door's knob turning. Immediately, she was flooded with dread. The previous night's events flashed around in her memory.

The door opened.

"Roger?" she said, almost breathlessly.

"You look like you've seen a ghost. What's the matter?"

"What are you doing here?" she asked, with confusion and fear on her face and in her voice. She stood to her feet once more and dusted off her pleated skirt.

"I called to tell you that I was going to come by today. Didn't you get my message?"

Alice looked over to the phone and saw the flashing light on the answering machine. Suddenly, the fear dissipated and she was left with only embarrassment. "Geez, I'm so sorry. I haven't checked it for a while. There's just been a lot going on."

"Don't worry about it. I probably

should have tried to call again before coming over, to be honest. Consider it my fault. Anyway, I fixed a couple of lights and patched a few holes," he said, with kindness in his voice. "Oh yeah, did you know about this?" He raised his thumb like a hitchhiker and pointed behind his shoulder to the door that he'd just walked through.

"Know about what?" she asked, confused.

"The lock's completely broken. It turns, but it doesn't actually engage."

Alice stared at him blankly and wondered how long it had been that way. She tried to remember if she had checked the knob after locking it the night before, or if she'd just turned the lock and blindly trusted it. She usually jiggled to be sure, but she had been in such a hurry. "I had no idea, actually," she replied, still surprised.

"I'll fix and then head on out. Let me know if I missed anything."

"Thanks." She rubbed a muscle in her forehead. "I appreciate the help."

"Oh, and Alice, thanks for helping my sister last night. She hasn't really been herself lately. I picked her up from the hospital this morning. She's doing okay, but, well, things have been hard for her for a little while."

"No problem. I understand completely. What was she doing here anyway?"

"Well, I'm sure you've heard that my niece, Sarah, used to live here."

Alice nodded.

"Betty had a little too much to drink, and I think she probably thought that Sarah was home or something. She has a really difficult time telling her dreams from reality when she's been drinking. I keep telling her to slow down on the bottles, but it's a new hobby of hers, I guess. If she shows up again, I mean, hopefully, she doesn't, but if she does, just give me a call and I'll come get her." He pulled his jeans up a little higher onto his large belly and sat down on the floor. He lifted a screwdriver from one of his deep pockets and started disassembling the doorknob.

"Okay, I'll definitely let you know if she comes by again." Alice turned and walked a few steps toward the living room, but suddenly stopped. "Hey, Roger..."

"Whatcha need, miss?"

She walked back into the kitchen and crouched down next to him. "Well, actually, could you tell me a little more about Sarah? I mean, if it's not uncomfortable for you to talk about. It's just that, well, I feel like I'm always hearing her name, but I don't know much about her at all."

He sat his screwdriver down and looked into Alice's eyes as if he was searching for something in them. A drop of dirty sweat dripped from his brow and down the side of his cheek, almost resembling a tear. He wiped it away, unintentionally increasing that resemblance, and cleared his throat. "She was a sweet girl," he said. "She loved her family, and everyone she met seemed to love her, too. She had these big brown eyes that could melt the heart of anyone who looked at them." He smiled for a moment before continuing with a more somber expression. "There was this guy who was absolutely taken by her. A lot of men liked Sarah, but this one was completely head-over-heels. He was actually the last known person to be seen with her, but when the cops questioned him, his alibi was completely solid."

"What? That's frightening. What was the alibi?" Alice asked, surprised at the direction the conversation was already taking.

"He claimed that he had been at Kirt's Pub all night, and he had the receipts and witnesses to prove it. I still don't feel right about the guy, but there's nothing I can do about it now."

"Oh... I see. Did Sarah like him, too?

Or was it more of a one-sided thing? Sorry if I'm asking too many questions. I can mind my own business if —"

"She liked him at first," he continued. "I think so, anyway. They'd gone on a few dates, but then she let him down. He didn't seem to handle the rejection very well, and he called her a lot after that. I remember stopping by to fix her sink one day, and he called five times that hour."

"Five times in an hour? That's ridiculous! Why did she meet up with him that last time?"

"I'm not sure. He had claimed that they were still friends and would still go out sometimes, but it all just seemed so weird to me. It still does, actually. The look that she had on her face each time he called — that was enough for me to know that they weren't friends. People aren't afraid of their friends."

"Yeah, that doesn't sound good at all..." she replied, with her voice trailing off sympathetically.

"I've even been thinking about getting my hair cut at Edna's and dealing with all of the perm fumes to avoid seeing his face as much. Just the sight of that guy makes my blood boil. I know I can't completely avoid him, but that might help a little bit, you know?"

"Wait — what do you mean by that?" she asked, confused.

"Oh, he's one of the barbers over at Pete's. Goes by Benji."

Chapter 7

"Like A Prayer"

Roger drove through the streets a little faster than usual, rolling past each of the rusty sun-faded stop signs. He cranked the driver's side window down and stuck his left arm out. His hand played with the breeze as he made his way to the edge of town. The tiny moisture-loving bugs smacked into his palms as he approached the lakeside house. He knew that Betty would be home, and he was determined to have a conversation with her while she was still sober. The sun was going down, which meant that her bottles would soon be rising up.

When he had dropped her off at the house after she'd been discharged, he had been in too much of a hurry to go inside and check on things. He had only spared enough time to feed the pigs before hurrying away again. There was a little bit of guilt in the back of his mind for not making sure she had everything that she needed, and for not at least going in to see if Will was doing okay. Roger's brother definitely wasn't supposed to be alone for extended periods of time, but he was more than capable of at least heating food up by himself. He justified the negligence by assuming that at the very worst, Will might only need to be told to bathe. He had a bad habit of playing with the pigs and not washing their muddy shit off of his clothes afterward.

"A night of dirty clothes won't hurt him," he thought, reassuring himself, as he turned into the long and winding driveway. *"It might even toughen him up a little. People treat him like a child, but he's a grown-ass man. He's a little strange, sure, but he's completely capable of taking a shower on his own. He shouldn't have to be*

told to do something like that."

The car's tires kicked up several pieces of gravel while it traveled along the curve to the back of the house. Roger put his foot down heavily onto the brake. He didn't bother to straighten out the steering wheel before cutting the engine. Daylight was coming to an end, and there was no time left to lose. With more of a gallop than a walk, his feet hurried across the driveway and made their way to the back porch. He knocked twice out of courtesy, and then let himself inside with the spare key from under the flower pot.

The house smelled strong inside, like paint thinner, old urine, and stale cigarette smoke. Somewhere all mixed in was the smell of rancid meat. Betty must have left pork out to thaw again, and forgot about it completely. It wouldn't have been the first time. It probably wouldn't be the last time either. Roger coughed into his arm and held back the urge to gag. The last thing the house needed was a new smell mixing in.

The lights were off, and there was no one in the living room. He headed in the direction of the kitchen and turned the wiggly plastic knob on a table-side lamp while passing by. The dim yellow light illuminated a trail of empty wine bottles and broken picture frames. The trail led up to a small mountain of trash bags, and the intrusive buzzing of flies became more obvious to his ears. He coughed again and opened the curtain by the table. The disaster became a lot more visible in what was left of the sunshine.

He turned, and his eyes met what was left of Sarah's. The picture, red with paint and wine, was evidence of Betty's mental decline. "Dammit. Betty!" His face reddened to match the one before him on the canvas. "You'd better get down here right now!"

He knocked the easel over with the back of his hand. Footsteps scurried on the floor above him and eventually made their way to the stairs. Betty scuttled over each step, wearing a blue moth-eaten nightgown. The gown was wrinkled and stained from an assortment of mysterious spills. Her hair was a mess, and it became very obvious that she'd been asleep the entire day.

"What the hell is that?" Roger yelled, pointing to the painting on the floor. "Is that supposed to be Sarah or something?"

His sister sobbed and leaned against the handrail at the bottom. She didn't use words to reply, but her reaction was enough to confirm his suspicion.

"She's gone, Betty," he said, scolding her. "You need to get a hold of yourself! She's not coming back, and even if she somehow did, what would she think if she saw that you were behaving like this? You've been acting like a crazy person!"

"I know she's gone. And you're right! She's not coming back!" Betty's voice broke into louder sobs, and she fell to the floor.

Roger's posture grew less aggressive, and he knelt down beside her. "Dammit. I'm sorry. I shouldn't have said that. She's gotta be out there somewhere, but we can't keep our lives paused while we wait for answers. We have to keep going." He looked around the room again. "We can't keep sitting around, getting as drunk as skunks, painting weird pictures, and scaring every person in town. You have a business to run. No one is going to want to buy meat from the town lunatic. You scared that poor girl half to death. You're hurting my business now too, you know."

Betty looked up and nodded. "I feel really bad about going to Alice's house," she mumbled.

"Well, you probably should. I was just over there, and she seems really jumpy." Roger stood up and helped Betty to her feet. His hands patted her shoulders as if he were dusting the sadness away, and he pulled her in for a comforting hug. "Sorry for yelling. Things will get better. Just promise me, no more drinking, okay?"

She looked to the floor like a child.

"Fine. No more drinking."

"Good. Now, where's Will?"

"I'm not sure… He's been outside all day again, I think."

***

Will strolled through town early that morning, taking his usual path, pulling a red wagon along with him to collect things to recycle. He was taller than average, about 6' 2" and surprisingly stocky, considering all of the walking that he did. His gray-blonde hair was slightly receded, and the thin spots revealed a sun-burnt scalp underneath. An old belt, clearly too large for him, held his jeans tightly under his belly due to the additional holes that had been added in to make it stay on. The extra leather hung by his pocket, wobbling with each step that he'd take.

He grunted and muttered as he made his way past the little shops and houses. Most of the words that fell out from his mouth were just random phrases that he had heard on the TV or radio earlier that day, but he occasionally grumbled about the assortment of things that were bothering him. At the time, he had been very annoyed with the food choices at Betty's.

"Pork sandwiches. I'm so sick of all of these damn sandwiches." He stopped walking for a few seconds and stared at Medley's. "Damn sandwiches."

He started moving again and headed into the store. He had a very specific route, even among the groceries. A few faces smiled at him when he passed by, but the people knew not to bother him with much more than that. He smiled back inwardly, but his facial expressions didn't mirror the feeling very well. His brow wore a seemingly permanent scowl.

Will walked over to the bread section and started to organize his favorite kind, Wonderbread. He picked up each loaf individually and stacked them on top of each other, one by one, with accuracy. The other loaves were left alone. They didn't even matter to him. The Wonderbread, however, was his deity, and his hands were there to worship. Unlike many churchgoers who only attended services weekly, Will organized the bread daily. When the yeasty smell filled his nostrils, visions of his mother flashed around in his head, and he momentarily escaped into one of the scenes.

"Now, William, you'd better eat enough bread if you want to grow big and strong. Here, this is the best kind you can get in the whole entire world. It's just like chewing on a cloud." His eyes were closed,

and he reached around blindly to grab another loaf off of the pile in front of him, picturing himself grabbing the soft plastic bag of bread from his mother's hands. "Yes, Mama," he said out loud.

He continued to stand in the aisle for several seconds with the same loaf still in his grip. His mother's brown hair and loose modest dresses continued to fill his mind. A smile spread all the way across his face as he imagined her wiping the mess of jam from his mouth with a raggedy dish rag. He could almost smell the old water that had mildewed in its fibers. *"You're a good boy, William. Let's get another piece of toast for you,"* he recalled her saying.

To the onlookers, the townspeople, Will was just an oddball who always obsessed over little things. He'd been a little unusual since the baseball accident with his brother, Roger, but he was typically friendly and well-behaved. There was no denying that he was noticeably different than everyone else, but he never caused any problems. He was very passive, and sadly, usually the victim of taunting. Even though he had once been a sharp young boy, with a mind as bright as his snow-colored hair, something changed in his brain after the baseball bat had smacked him in the head. He was still highly intelligent. He just spoke less, obsessed more, and had little moments where he would lose clarity.

Sometimes Will's dreams were indiscernible from reality, and this annoyance occasionally caused problems for him. Other than a personality change though, he was still very much his old and original self. But sadly, even in his forties, he wasn't able to escape the playground bullies. New generations carried on the tradition of torment after the previous ones had matured and lost interest.

He finished his ritual, exchanged a nod with Jim near the register, and went on his way out of the door. A woman passed by, and he sheepishly waved.

"Oh, hi there, Will. How are you doing today?" she asked, kindly returning the wave.

Will shifted uncomfortably and stared at the woman's feet. "I'm good. What size shoes do you wear?"

The woman looked down, confused by the abrupt change of subject, and then met his eyes again. "Uh, These are a 7, I think. I usually wear a 7 or 7 ½. Why do you want to know all that, Will?"

"My mom wore size 7. She liked pretty shoes like yours."

"That's very sweet of you to think of her, Will. Judy would be so proud of the thoughtful and caring man you've become." She spoke to him as if he were a child, despite him being fully capable of having an adult conversation.

Will was used to it. He grinned, still staring at her shoes. "Can I have them?" he asked.

"Well, I mean, I need them right now. I can't go walking around the store barefoot, now, can I?" she replied, chuckling at the thought.

Will didn't respond.

"How about this," she began. "I need to clear out some of my old things anyway. I'll go through my shoes tonight, and I'll set some pretty ones out on the porch for you to pick up. You know which house is mine, don't you? The little blue one over on Third."

"Thank you, Ma'am," he said, with a smile replacing his typically-serious expression.

"Sure thing. Now, you take care, okay?"

"Okay, you too," he said flatly and continued walking again.

He made a loop around the parking lot and decided to head back in the direction of his house. A lot had been accomplished during that trip, and he didn't feel the need to wander much more after such a huge success. He pulled his wagon along, in the direction of the lake. After passing through a few of the usual streets, a small group of boys, appearing to range in age from seven to ten confronted him. Each of their taunting voices pierced his ears like knives.

"Hey, it's Wonderbread Will! I heard that Elvis doesn't really sing his own songs! He just mouths them out on stage!"

The boys giggled together.

"Yeah! He can't really dance either! He just puts ants in his pants and wiggles around!"

"He dyes his hair like a chick!" yet another voice chimed in, higher in pitch than the others.

Will froze in place and listened angrily while the boys insulted his favorite musician. He clenched his fists and tears welled in his eyes. From the late 50s until a couple of years before, he and his mother would sit and listen to Elvis together each evening. From the way that Will's mother had spoken to him about the singer, it was reasonable to assume that Elvis was the closest thing to a father in Will's life. She would often make up stories about him, and how he was going to visit Will one day. After his mother's voice had faded into the earth, he was still able to hear Elvis's. Those songs were as precious to him as his memories.

"Guess what else!" the tallest of the

boys called out.

"No, don't do it. He looks like he's getting really mad," another boy whispered nervously, nudging the tall one with a bony elbow.

"Just watch. It'll be funny," he said, pushing back. He cupped his hands around his mouth, preparing to project his voice. "Elvis is dead! Just like your Ma!" he yelled.

Will shook with an overwhelming amount of emotion. He let out a loud and painful groan in protest. As quickly as he could move, his feet darted toward the boys, and they all took off running down the sidewalk. "They're not dead!" he yelled, "They're not dead, you little shits!"

Tears streamed down his face as he chased after the group. After a couple of blocks, the boys had completely outrun him, and he slowed down to catch his breath. He wiped his face with the hem of his shirt and retrieved his wagon that he'd knocked over into the ditch. Will walked the rest of the way home, humming songs as if nothing had happened at all.

The boys laughed together in the distance.

Chapter 8

"Sweet Dreams"

The wind howled and whistled through Wintersburg. April had come to a close, and May's unpredictability was fresh upon the land. The warm air pushed itself through the trees and past the small cracked buildings, forcing what was left of the cold to hide away in the safety of the night.

Alice flopped around in her bed,

tangling and untangling herself with the sheets. Her hair was moist with sweat, and the discomfort of it eventually caused her to wake up. She walked over to the bedroom window and opened it a few inches. The chilly breeze rushed inside as if it were running away from something, but she welcomed it into her home with a big sigh of gratitude.

She rested in front of the window, with her hands combing through her hair. The earth's natural blow dryer blew the sweat away from her scalp, and her eyes grew too heavy to keep open any longer. She told herself that she'd only close them for a minute — she just had to finish cooling off first. The wind continued to feather across her skin, and it eventually lulled her back to sleep.

Something tickled the tiny hairs on her arm, and she opened her eyes slowly. Each pupil scoured the room for answers, searching for some type of a new presence. On her bed, she saw the blurry figure of a woman, lying in what was supposed to be her place.

Alice rubbed the sleep from her eyes and looked once more, unsure of whether or not she was dreaming. The color of the sheets was different, and the bed was too, but the girl definitely looked a lot like her, at least from where Alice was sitting. *"If I'm right here, how can I be over there?"*

Her eyes wandered across the room again. There were paintings and posters, none of which were her own. Her vanity and chair were missing, and they had been replaced with a different version of the pair. The white paint chipped from the wood around the mirror.

In a quick flash, bright orange sunlight suddenly flooded the room from the window behind her. She jumped and gasped, but stayed put. The bed creaked next to her, and she saw the woman switching positions over and over again. She seemed to be waking from an unpleasant dream.

The woman rolled around uncomfortably in the sheets, just as Alice had done earlier. A loud yawn escaped from her mouth, and she sat upright in the bed. Her arms raised into the air for a big stretch, before falling down lightly to her sides, startling Alice. She lifted the sheets from her body and placed a pair of bare feet on the ground, one by one.

Alice was able to get a better look at the woman's face.

"Wait, that's not me... That's — that's Sarah!" Her heart beat harder and faster until she could feel her pulse throbbing in her forehead. Music burst in, spewing from the boombox in the corner of the room.

Sarah danced around the room, singing into a hairbrush. The sun played in her long brown hair, and she spun and twirled all around, jumping onto the bed and then back down to the floor. She made exaggerated poses with her makeshift microphone in the reflection of the mirror. After a few minutes that only seemed like seconds, Sarah dug around in a drawer and pulled out a cassette tape. She skipped over to the boombox and switched out an old tape for the new one. She pushed the clunky button down with one of her long fingernails, rewinded the tape to the very beginning, and then pressed Play.

Before any more music could come out of the speakers, an uncomfortable crinkling sound filled the air. Sarah pushed Stop as quickly as she could, and opened the cassette player to examine the problem. The stereo kept playing anyway and the rollers continued to turn the tape wheels even though it had been opened. A long winding strip of plastic began to crawl out from the cassette's rectangular shell. The black ribbon seemed to have no end as it twisted and wrapped itself around everything in the room, climbing the table legs and lamp posts like dark and angry vines. Sarah stepped back and dropped her hairbrush on the ground. The heavy handle thudded next to her, but she didn't react to the sound. Her face grew very pale as she stared in horror at the boombox, but then she turned to face Alice.

A cloud must have passed by because the sunlight dimmed a lot at that moment. Sarah opened her mouth as if she were waiting on words to come out, but not a single one managed to escape from the orifice. She looked into Alice's eyes and opened her mouth even wider. She was determined. This time, it looked more like she was trying to scream, but still, her voice was silent. A thin dark line streamed down her chin and neck, followed by more and more lines.

Alice jumped up to help but froze in her tracks when she realized what was happening.

Tape curled out of Sarah's mouth and wrapped itself around her throat. It squeezed her tightly, like some sort of an anorexic python, and caused the color to go back into her cheeks. There was far too much color though — her face had turned a disconcerting shade of purple. She yanked at the tape, trying desperately to slip her fingers in the space between the plastic and her neck, but she had very little success. Had it only circled around once or twice, she could have been able to break it. She reached a hand out to Alice, with her eyes begging for help. They reddened from several bursting blood vessels.

Alice lunged toward her, pulling and clawing at the tape. Just as she finally began to make progress in freeing Sarah's throat, the tape completely disappeared. She looked all around, searching for evidence that anything had even happened, but not even a fragment of evidence remained. She panted loudly and placed Sarah's cold hand between both of hers.

"What's happening right now? Are you okay?" she asked with tangible fear in her voice.

Silence.

"Sarah, please tell me what's going on," she begged, pausing to inhale sharply. "What are you doing here? We need to tell someone that you're back!"

More silence.

Sarah stood there motionlessly as if she were nothing more than a plastic store mannequin. After a few seconds of completely vacant eyes and paralyzed lungs, she moved to open her mouth once more. It was much less agape than before. Again, she looked as if she were about to speak, but she just stared off into the distance instead. Finally, from the slight parting of her lips, something else came out — something not quite audible.

Powdery brown dirt fell out of Sarah's

mouth and onto the floor in puffs from each of her short breaths.

The brown powder eventually turned into dark damp clumps, filled with broken dandelions and worms. They moved erratically as if they'd just been injected with epinephrine. A few of the creatures crawled wildly up her cheeks and toward her ears, where they eventually burrowed themselves into her eardrums. An especially large worm wriggled itself up above her lip. It shot up her nose and lifted the flesh under her eyes as it traveled through her sinuses. As a result of its voyage, red liquid dripped from one of Sarah's tear ducts. The tiny hole ripped wider, into more of a slit, and the large worm appeared from the wound. It glided across her eye and nestled its head beneath the lid. Sarah's entire eye seemed to completely dissolve beneath its slimy body, and her other eye vanished as well. More worms curled upward out of her mouth and buried themselves into the newly empty sockets.

Sarah abruptly snapped to life. She blindly darted out of the room and into the hallway, spitting dirt and worms all around. She left a trail of them behind, like Hansel and Gretel, but her intentions of returning were unknown. A foul stench penetrated the air. It was something that could have only been compared to a mixture of roadkill and stagnant swampy water.

Alice hurried to chase after her, but she accidentally stomped and smeared the large earthworms all around the flooring beneath her soles. She called out while leaving the bedroom, but was ignored. One of the worms was a little more well-fed than the others, and it caused Alice to slip as her heel made contact with its body. Juices rubbed themselves all over her ankles, and she suppressed a gag.

She realized that she couldn't see or hear Sarah anymore, so she searched all around the hallway floor. Slowly this time, she crept along the piles of worms and dirt, taking care to avoid the earthy mess, and followed the trail into the bathroom. She hadn't expected to walk into a scene like this one though. Really, she hadn't even known what to expect, but it definitely wasn't this.

Sarah's body sat mangled on the floor like a melted Barbie doll. Her neck was bruised and swollen, and her face was pale and drained of color again, aside from the bluish-purple smudges beneath her eyes. Her hair had been chopped away carelessly and close to the scalp in some places. Strands and chunks of it were flung all over the place, some held together in clusters by small puddles of bright red blood that littered the floor.

She didn't try to move anymore.

***

Alice screamed and jumped awake. She was still on the floor where she'd accidentally fallen asleep. The wind whipped papers around in her room and sent chills all across her body. She wiped the cold sweat from her forehead and turned around to close the window. Everything looked normal again. There were no signs of broken cassettes, worms, dirt, or even of Sarah. All of the furniture and decorations were her own again. She peeked her head into the hallway, but the floor was as clean as it had been when she'd gotten home that night.

Nothing had happened.

She climbed into bed and wrapped herself back up in the sheets. *"It was just a bad dream,"* she assured herself. *"It was only a dream."*

Chapter 9

"Predator"

Benji stood in front of Medley's, jingling the change in his pocket. He paced back and forth as he stared at the soda machines, trying to make a choice. His favorite orange drink had been sold out for a while, and he wasn't exactly adjusting well to the change.

These vending machine trips were a big part of his regular shopping routine. Each fizzy drink seemed to provide him with a bit of a sugary escape during his drives back home. They were his way of zesting up the monotony of grocery shopping.

He sighed and settled for a cola, cracking it open after sliding his grocery bags up into the bend of his arms. A long swig filled his mouth, and he gulped with obnoxious exaggeration.

"Ahhhh," he exhaled, loudly.

He wiped the fizz from his mouth and turned to face the bulletin board. His eyes instantly focused on the Missing poster, and he stood there grinning in between smaller sips from his frosty can. After a few seconds, he reached one of his hands up to touch the photocopied picture of Sarah. The other women's photos were ignored by his fingers, but Sarah's face received all of his affection. Benji slowly licked his lips and closed his eyes as he brought his hand back down to his side once more. The grocery bags slid down his forearm. His mind was shocked back to reality. He caught the bags before they could hit the ground, but ended up dropping his cola instead. The entirety of the contents poured out and foamed against the concrete.

"Dammit!"

He kicked the aluminum can and

walked over to his '84 Rx-7. The car's white paint reflected the sunlight back toward him, so he looked down at the ground to shield his eyes as he unlocked the door. After placing his grocery bags into the passenger's seat, he crouched inside and shut the door. The burgundy leather was hot against his skin, but he adjusted to the warmth quickly and lit up a cigarette. He rolled the window down and blew out a gust of smoke. His body relaxed the rest of the way into the seat, and his mind drifted off into a daydream. He imagined Sarah's face, and within seconds, memories of their past dates came rushing back to him.

He could see her, with a pouty frown on her face, standing in front of him in a yellow top and a faded jean skirt. Her hair had a yellow bow tucked into her bangs to match the outfit. She looked so precious to him in that moment, which is exactly why he had burned every single detail of the encounter into his brain. Even when she had smacked him across the face, he had smiled back at her, chuckling lightly, squeezing her cheeks between his pointer finger and thumb, and then shaking her skull violently until she cried. He left two bruises on her face in the place of dimples.

"My God, she looked beautiful that day."

He laughed out loud and tossed the

last bit of his cigarette out the window.

***

Alice spent her morning and afternoon off work in the library. It was smaller than the one she usually visited in Parkington, but it felt more unique and special. The air was scented by the baked goods that the librarians had brought in. They had been trying to sell cakes and cookies to fund new reader's programs. Alice decided that a few sugary treats couldn't hurt anything, so she bought an enviable assortment.

"I won't tell anyone if you decide to eat a few in here," the elderly woman's voice creaked out from behind the makeshift booth. "You're too thin to wait 'til later anyway. You'll turn into bones if you don't get some dough in your stomach soon." She followed the statement with a wink.

Alice giggled and returned the wink. "I guess I could use a little fattening, huh? I promise not to leave any crumbs behind," she said while handing over a few singles.

The woman smiled and accepted the bills. "Thanks so much, young lady."

Alice nodded warmly and turned to browse for a few more minutes. She ate one of the sugar cookies while walking around, and then decided that it was time to head on home again. From the window, she could tell that it was going to start raining soon, so she gathered her treats, stuffed them all into her purse, and made her way outside. Hoping to beat the rain, she walked faster than usual, but she still had several blocks to go before she could reach her house.

Not even a minute had passed by before small droplets of rain started to hit her on the head. They grew more abundant and large in size as she continued onward. Thunder roared in the distance, and the sky darkened more and more with each passing second.

A white car approached her from behind and flashed its lights. It pulled up next to her, and she heard a familiar voice call out from the opened window.

"Hey, get in! I'll take ya where you need to go."

She saw a hand waving to her, motioning for her to walk in its direction, so she crept toward the car door, slowly and cautiously.

"Benji? Oh, thank God. I'm getting soaked out here." She hopped in and buckled herself up. "I'm just heading home. Do you think you could drop me off there? It's over on Fifth," she asked as she began to rummage around for something in her purse.

"Not a problem. Edna mentioned that you're staying in Sarah's old place. I know exactly where that is."

"Oh, yeah, I'm pretty sure the whole town knows where I live by now. Word really travels fast apparently." She rolled her eyes at the thought of never having any privacy and pulled out a paper tissue. Mascara had smudged under her lashes from the rain, so she had wanted to buff it away. She looked out the window, and then back to Benji. "Hey, you just passed my place," she said, pointing.

"Yeah, I know. I was hoping we could get something to eat together first. You never called me after I left you my number, so I figured that we could get to know each other in person instead." He gripped the steering wheel tightly and smirked with confidence.

"Oh, sorry about that. I've been really busy lately, and need to get back home. Can't you just drop me off at my house and maybe we can meet up another time or —"

"You're so pretty," he interrupted. He lifted a hand and brushed her hair away from her shoulder. His fingers tickled across her collarbone, sending chills down the back of her neck and spine.

She smacked his hand away in protest.

"Whoa, what do you think you're doing right now?"

The car slowed down, and Benji pulled off on the side of the road. The rain poured all around and tapped angrily against the windshield.

"Sorry. Just listen to me for a second. I'm not trying to force you to go on a date with me. I'm just really attracted to you. I have been ever since I saw you at Edna's. Can't you at least have some cocoa with me? Something?" He pointed to the two cups of cocoa squeezed tightly between his thighs. "The cafe messed up my order and accidentally put whipped cream in the first one, so now I have two."

Alice sighed and reached out her hand. "Fine. We'll sip some here and talk, but then I'm going home whether you drop me off or if I have to walk back in the rain, okay?"

Benji nodded and handed her one of the cups.

"Why'd you even stop for cocoa anyway? It's May."

"Well, I was thirsty after grocery shopping. Cocoa is good no matter what time of year it is. It's not just for winter." He took a sip and looked up at her. "See, it even pairs well with the rain."

Alice shook her head and sipped from

her cup too. She returned his gaze and smiled automatically when the chocolate and whipped cream coated her tongue. It was difficult to stay annoyed when something tasted so good.

"So, what do you want to talk about so badly?" she asked.

"There's nothing specific. I'd just like to get to know you better... to hear what your life was like in Parkington, what brought you out here to Wintersburg — those sort of things."

Alice took a long drink and gulped hard. "Well, I was a hairdresser in Parkington too. Really, I did the same things I do here, but just in another place. It was only me and my grandma for a long time."

She paused to clear her throat, and Benji motioned for her to take another sip, which she did.

"My grandma passed a little while before I moved out here. She was originally from this town, so I just thought I'd see what it was like."

"Oh, so you're trying to learn more about her past, or...?"

"I really don't know. I think I just wanted to be close to her in some way again."

Benji nodded. "That makes sense," he

said as he brought his cup back up to his mouth. "I know what it's like to miss someone. Sometimes it feels good to be near the same things that they used to love." He sat his cup between his thighs again and rubbed the stubble around his jaw. His lips pursed as if he had thought of something unpleasant, and he started the car back up. "Anyway, let's get you home, I guess. The cocoa's almost gone, and I'm a man of my word."

Alice smiled and looked out the window again. Her house came into view as they turned back onto Fifth street, and she slung her purse back onto her shoulder. She felt Benji reach toward her and grab the cup from her hand after he had shifted in neutral.

"Oh, it's okay. I can throw it away when I get inside," she said, reaching for the cup again.

"No, it's fine. I'll toss it when I get home."

Confused by his insistence, but still agreeable, Alice shrugged and opened the car door. She stepped out onto the wet sidewalk and shielded the top of her head with her hands while the purse hung clumsily from her shoulder. "Thanks again!" she called back to him.

Benji rolled the window down once more. "Do you want me to walk you to the door?" he shouted.

Alice looked behind her, even more confused. The house was only a few feet from the road. "Uh... I think I can handle it. I'll see ya around, I'm sure!"

He nodded with a frown and looked back at the road. The wheels of his car turned, and he drove away into the rainy night.

Alice stepped inside the house and locked the door. There was something strange about that man, but she still couldn't figure out what it was. He seemed overly assertive, or even aggressive, but also... friendly?

"Maybe I'm reading him wrong," she thought. *"Maybe I'm the one who's being weird."*

She headed into the kitchen and sat her purse on the counter to unload her library snacks. Seeing all of the baked goods again made her stomach growl, so she decided to make a late lunch. After all, she hadn't eaten a real meal all day. Her hand reached ahead and she grabbed the refrigerator door to reveal what was inside.

"Milk. Eggs. Cheese. Old takeout."

She grabbed the carton of fried rice that had been bought two nights before. She opened the flaps and looked inside, sniffing the contents.

"This will have to do, I guess."

She popped the carton into the microwave and leaned against the counter, waiting for the food to heat up. The lights flickered a few times. The microwave buzzed strangely, suddenly unable to properly produce currents, and it ceased to function. Just as quickly, the room went dark, and the power went out in the entire house.

Alice cursed the house's electrical issues as she made her way down the basement stairs with a flashlight. Usually, it was only one or two rooms that would lose power at a time, so she was more frustrated than ever. The breaker was one of the only things in the basement that had remained dust-free due to all of the attention it had been getting since she had moved in. It seemed like every few days, something would cause it to kick, and she would have to go down the stairs to reset it again.

She flipped the switch off and on and everything became bright once more. While turning to go back up the stairs, the cardboard box in the corner caught her attention again, so she walked toward it instead. Her hands fumbled around with the top for a moment, and she batted a few cobwebs out of the way. She reached inside and sat a stack of photographs in her lap.

There were still a lot of things in the box, but she decided that she'd look through those things later. Sarah's face had been haunting her thoughts ever since that strange dream, and she needed to see it smiling and lively again to shake the tainted images away. The top few photos were the ones that she'd already seen. She continued to go through them and placed each one on the floor beside her after it had been examined.

A photo of Betty made its way to the top of the stack. Alice was surprised to see a well-kempt and happy looking woman staring back at her. Betty's short black hair was curled and teased nicely. She wore a pair of white sunglasses on top of her head like a headband, pulling all of her hair back except for the fluffy feathered bangs that covered her forehead. A blue swimsuit clung to her body, paired with bright white cotton shorts, and a smile was cemented across her face, from cheek to cheek. Sarah was standing next to her, with one of her arms wrapped tightly across her mother's shoulder. She wore a loose floral sundress, and her only accessory was a short silver necklace.

Alice moved on to the next photo. This one showed only Sarah, and it had been taken much closer up than the previous one. The necklace was a lot clearer than before. Its silver chain shined with tiny embedded crystals. A pale lavender pendant sparkled as the light hit the glossy paper, and Alice recognized it immediately as the one that Grandma Susan used to wear.

She jumped up, still holding the photo, and accidentally dropped the remaining ones to the floor. They dispersed like dry autumn leaves. There was an older picture of her grandma in her wallet upstairs, and she wanted to compare the two necklaces in the photos side by side to confirm. The jewelry had been a wedding gift from her grandma's father, so it would have been really strange, or even impossible, for Sarah to have owned the same one.

"Surely, there has to be some sort of difference between them."

Once to her feet, she took a few steps forward toward the stairs. The floor began to wobble in front of her, and it felt as if she were standing upright on a small boat in a large and angry sea. Her hand reached out beside her, and she tried to steady her weight against the cold concrete wall.

"What's happening?" she wondered as she scaled the wall the rest of the way to the stairs.

She dropped to her knees and started to crawl up each creaky piece of wood instead. Even with her eyes closed, she could feel the room spinning and curving. Still, she continued up the steps, one by one, reaching ahead of herself, carefully. Just as her knees had passed over the third step from the bottom, a thin piece of wood shoved itself inside of her palm. Instinctively, she brought it up to her chest and her other hand let go to apply pressure to wound. In a panic, she raised to her feet, and her body grew even more unsteady than before.

She felt herself floating along the room's current. Only air was beneath her at that moment, until she crashed to the floor like a wave hitting the side of a cliff.

Her eyes closed and opened multiple times as she tried to get them to focus on something, on anything. She rolled over onto her back and looked up toward the top of the stairs. In between blinks, she was able to make out the looming silhouette of someone tall staring down at her from the kitchen.

Her eyes closed one more time.

Chapter 10
"Clue"

Alice woke to find Tiffany crouching above her, slapping her frantically and repeatedly in the face. Her red hair shined like a brand new penny beneath the yellow-toned basement lights. She tried to lift her arms to stop the smacking but stopped when she felt her shoulders aching. Her back felt like it was a single gigantic bruise.

"Come on! Hey!" Tiffany yelped as she tapped against Alice's cheeks. "Alice, wake up!"

Alice pushed through the discomfort and finally managed to swat one of the hands away from her face. She groaned and turned her head to look beside her. The photo of Sarah, wearing the necklace, was within reach, so she grabbed it out of fear of losing or damaging it in any way.

"You're awake. Oh goodness, I thought you'd died or something." Tiffany leaned back and sat cross-legged on the floor. Her sneakers were caked in dirt and mud as if she'd been working outside the entire day. A loud exhale escaped from her mouth, and she sighed even more while she ran her hands through her messy hair.

"How'd you get in here?" Alice asked with a groggy sleep-filled voice. "I thought I locked the door."

"Uh, no you didn't. That's exactly why I ran over here. Your back door was wide open."

"Wait, what?"

"Yeah. I was in my yard, pulling dandelions from the flowerbed and looked up at your place. Your door was open, so I walked over and called for you to see what you were up to. You didn't answer. I guess I got worried or something, so I went into the kitchen and saw that the basement door was wide open too. And there you were, at the bottom of the steps." She looked around, still uncomfortable with the entire situation. "Did you just fall or something? I mean, like, are you okay?" she asked.

Alice sat up slowly, moaning uncomfortably as she used her arms to straighten her posture. She faced Tiffany and mirrored her cross-legged pose. "I — I really don't know what happened. I think I'm okay though..." She looked around the basement to confirm that her vision was back to normal, and then continued answering the questions. "I came down here to reset the breaker, but then I got really dizzy when I tried to go back up. The room was spinning like crazy, like I was really drunk or something. I made it up a few of the steps but fell backward, I think." She rubbed her forehead, hoping to dull the pain of the lingering headache.

"You didn't hit your head, did you?"

"No, I don't think so. It hurts, but not like that."

Tiffany leaned in and looked directly into Alice's eyes. "You wait right here, okay? Don't try to go up the stairs again or anything. I'm going to call the cops and —"

"No, don't call them. They'll just take me to the hospital, and I really don't want to deal with that right now. I'll be fine. I just have a few bruises."

"Well, we can't just act like nothing happened. You said your doors were locked when you came down here. Obviously, someone or something had to open them."

Alice nodded, agreeing. "You're right. Let's not make a scene though. The people around here already have enough to talk about. If you go look at the fridge, Detective Darrow's number is there under a magnet. Give him a call and see if he can stop by."

"You're sure you don't need an ambulance?"

"I'm sure."

"Okay, I'll be back in a minute then. Don't budge."

Tiffany ran upstairs, and Alice put her head in her hands. She tried to remember the details of exactly what had happened before the fall, but everything was fuzzy.

***

Alice could hear Detective Darrow's

voice coming from the living room, along with the familiar sound of his boots hitting the floor. She had disregarded Tiffany's command to stay put and lifted her bruised bones up each step. It was a much easier task now that she had clear vision again, even with a headache. Once at the top, she peeked around the corner and into the kitchen to check the time.

6:00 PM.

"How had three hours gone by since I got home? Was I really asleep down there that long?" she wondered.

Her head continued to throb. She took a few more quiet steps into the kitchen and then dropped to her knees. A sharp high-pitched ringing sound stabbed her eardrums, practically immobilizing her for a moment. She looked up and saw Tiffany and Detective Darrow hurrying in her direction. Through the ringing, she could tell from their voices that they were very concerned.

"Alice! I told you to stay down there. You could have fallen again!" Tiffany yelled as she stooped down to the floor to grab Alice's shoulders.

Detective Darrow clicked a tiny flashlight on and lifted Alice's head up by the chin. He shined the light across her eyes several times, back and forth. He kept his hand there until she eventually pulled away.

"Alice?" he asked, with deep concern in his voice.

Instead of answering, she brought herself up on all fours and heaved onto the kitchen tiles. Brown froth poured out all over the floor and onto her hands. It seeped along the lines of grout and made its way to her knees. She heaved again, and again until several ounces of foamy liquid had covered the tile around her.

Tiffany jumped back and raised herself to her feet to escape the mess. Detective Darrow's instincts were different though. He wrapped his arms around Alice's waist and pulled her up to his chest. His bare hands pushed her wet brown hair away from her face, and he yelled over to Tiffany.

"Grab some towels and meet me in the bathroom! We need to get her cooled off."

Tiffany nodded and ran into the hallway to rummage for some in the closet. "I found a few!" she yelled back to him.

Detective Darrow stood up and bent down into a squatting position. He lifted Alice up to her feet and wrapped one of her arms across his shoulder and neck to help support her weight. Slowly, he guided her out of the kitchen, through the hallway, and into the bathroom.

Her ears had stopped ringing, and she

felt defeated. "I'm so sorry," she whispered once they had reached the shower. "Oh God, this is so embarrassing."

"There's nothing to be embarrassed about. We just need you to feel better, okay?" He turned to look at Tiffany. "Help her if she needs it. Stay in here — I'll take care of the kitchen."

"Got it," she said, understanding his commands, and being annoyed by them at the same time. Of course, she was going to help Alice. She wasn't an idiot.

Detective Darrow grabbed a couple of the towels and shuffled out of the room.

Tiffany helped Alice into the shower and closed the curtain behind her. "Let me know if you need anything. I'll just wait here. You can have your privacy."

"Thanks, Tiff. I'm really okay. I think it's just a migraine or something. I used to get them when I was a teen. They've just never been this bad before."

"Hopefully that's all it is. I told the cop about the door though. He looked pretty worried."

"The landlord came over not too long ago and fixed the lock. I wonder if it broke again or something. Maybe it just flung open," Alice replied.

"Maybe, maybe not. I think Darrow is really eager to find out though. This is the most serious I've ever seen the guy."

"I remember something though. I'll show you when I finish getting this puke out of my hair," she said while she scrubbed the grime away. "I found a picture of Sarah down there —"

"Yeah? What picture?" Tiffany asked.

"It looked like she was on vacation with her mom. She had on a necklace that looked identical to the one my grandma used to wear."

"Lots of people have similar jewelry, Alice. There's only so much you can do to make a necklace look unique without turning it into a huge mess."

"I know, but this was an antique. It just seemed odd to me that she would have the same one. My grandma was from this town too, so I thought maybe they could have known each other somehow."

"I guess so. I wouldn't focus on that too much right now. We just need you to get better for now. Oh, how about this!" She clapped excitedly from the toilet seat. "You can stay over at my place tonight. We'll sit back, relax, eat some pizza... or uh... just crackers... and watch some movies. I'll go rent a few tapes after you get dressed!"

"Okay, that'd be nice. I'd rather not be alone right now anyway."

"Yeah, I kind of don't want to be either."

Alice finished her shower and reached for the towel. Tiffany guided her out of the tub to make sure she didn't slip and then went to the kitchen. She saw that Detective Darrow had cleaned everything up and had been pacing nervously next to a small pile of dirty towels.

"I checked the doors. It looks like something happened to the doorknob in the back. It didn't look like anyone tampered with it or anything though. The latch just won't engage. Anything could've pushed that thing open."

"She mentioned that her landlord came out to fix it a while ago."

"Well, he did a pretty bad job," Detective Darrow replied. "I'll run to the hardware store and get some things to replace it tonight."

Tiffany nodded. "I'm having her stay with me anyway. Just come over and knock when you're done."

"Alright. That sounds like a good plan."

The following morning, Alice felt much better. The bruises still lingered and her muscles felt pretty sore, but she was determined to make the best of the day. With Saturday gone, Sunday was all she had left until the work week started again. The Salon was closed on Sundays anyway, but Edna had compassion for the youthful and always gave her the full weekend off.

"Don't waste the best days of the week workin'," she'd told her when they had discussed an appropriate schedule. "You can't ask for your youth back once it leaves you, but money can always show up no matter how old you get."

Alice smiled at the thought. She grabbed her purse from the living room table and folded the blanket that she had used to keep warm. "Want me to put this anywhere in particular, or should I just toss it back on the couch?" she asked.

Tiffany shrugged from the quilted chair across the room and looked up from her magazine. "Don't worry about it. You can leave it wherever. I fall asleep over there while watching TV half of the time anyway."

Alice placed the blanket back on the couch and walked toward the front door. She checked her purse for her keys and gave a small wave in Tiffany's direction. "Thanks again for looking out for me. We should have a girls' night out soon. I think we could both use some drinks."

"That'd be nice. Just let me know what night works for you."

"Yep, will do! I'll talk to ya later then."

She waved again and Tiffany nodded before returning her attention back to the magazine in her lap. The sun beamed across Alice's skin, warming it slightly as she walked home. The breeze blew through her hair, and she felt like she was in one of those cheesy shampoo commercials for a moment — the ones where the women always had effortlessly fluffy hair and flawless sun-kissed complexions. She grinned at the thought.

She walked in through her front door and sat her purse down in the kitchen, as usual. The back door was shut and had a brand new deadbolt lock installed. Detective Darrow must have spent a decent amount of time working on it, making sure that there wouldn't be any more issues from then on. A little note had been left taped next to the knob, along with a new key.

Fixed the lock. Give me a call if you need anything else.

She grabbed the key and added it to the others on her key-ring, but left the note alone. Her eyes wandered around the kitchen and she took notice of how nicely it had been cleaned. It was as if nothing gross had happened at all. Mixed with the scent of lemon cleaning supplies, she picked up on the smell of laundry detergent. She walked down the basement stairs, following her nose. On the laundry table, her clothes from the day before, along with several towels, sat folded and clean.

"Holy cow. He cleaned everything! Well, almost."

Her eyes wandered back over to the box. The photos were still on the floor where they'd fallen the day before. She crept next to them and stacked everything together nicely. The box seemed even more inviting than before, and her curiosity was in full-force. She knelt down beside the box and started rummaging through the various trinkets, knickknacks, and other things. She picked up a yellow bow and twirled it around in her fingers, admiring it.

At the very bottom of the box, the heaviest item rested. It was a portable tape recorder, and a nice one too! Alice lifted it out and opened the tape deck. A cassette was still inside. She closed it and pressed the arrows to rewind it to the beginning, anxious and excited to see what was recorded. The batteries were dead, but a cord dangled from the back. Without wasting another moment, she shoved the yellow bow in her pocket and ran upstairs with the tape recorder.

She plugged it in one of the kitchen outlets and heard the tape whirring once she'd hit the button to rewind it again. It came to a stop, and she pressed play.

At first, there was static, and then some shuffling noises, as if someone's hands had been messing around with the microphone area. A few seconds of complete silence followed, but then it was interrupted by a voice.

"Sarah Noe, here. The date is November 17th, 1987. I'll be singing my favorite song for you today."

Alice listened while Sarah introduced herself to an imaginary audience. She listened even more intently when the narration turned into a song. She could tell that Sarah was just being goofy when she had recorded this, but it still felt nice to hear her happy and singing.

A loud thud, like a door slamming, came from the speaker, and Sarah's singing came to an abrupt stop. "What are you doing in here?" Sarah's voice had said, with anxiety in her tone. "I told you to stay out of my room."

A male voice replied to her. "I — I didn't mean to..."

Shuffling and footsteps could be heard, and then the sound of a door slamming. Sarah sighed into the microphone, and then the tape went completely silent.

Alice fast-forwarded to try to find more audio, but that was all that had been recorded. While it seemed like nothing, it still felt like something important. She unplugged the tape recorder and took it to her bedroom, figuring that it would be safer to keep it in her closet with her own personal belongings than to leave it alone in the basement.

"I'll bring the other things up here, too," she thought. *"They had been important to her at some point. I might as well take care of them in case she comes back."*

Chapter 11

"Moonlighting"

The rest of Alice's day off work was relaxing — something that was very much needed given all of life's changes for her as of late. A lot of her time had been spent flipping through the different TV channels, or snacking on things that she probably shouldn't have been eating in such large quantities, like candies, pastries, and even more takeout. Life had been so exhausting in those recent weeks, despite the transfer to a slower-paced environment. She wondered if her existence had always been so stressful, or if the chaos of the city had just made it all seem like nothing at the time, in comparison.

But no, that couldn't have been the case — at least not in entirety. While people went missing in the city too, the circumstances were definitely very different. Cities like Parkington were large and full of many people. People came and went all the time in places like that. Wintersburg, however, was a tiny blister of people who rarely multiplied, and who rarely died from anything other than old age, aside from the occasional car crash. When something was amiss, the problem was usually larger than their entire town.

Stress like this was new for her. Not only had all of these women been going missing from the narrow streets that she walked along daily — not only did she share a strong resemblance to those women — but she was also living in the house of the most recent possible victim. And, to make matters even worse, no one really had a clue as to why any of it was happening. The cops didn't have enough tips or evidence to connect any of the women to each other, so everything was at a standstill until something else happened. The whole thing was pretty much paused unless another body turned up, or even worse — until another woman happened to vanish.

That was more than enough to turn a person into an anxious mess.

Alice licked the grease from her fingertips and stepped into the kitchen. Detective Darrow had crossed her mind a few times, and she had been thinking of different ways to thank him for all of his help. She was still absolutely riddled with embarrassment, but she owed it to him to at least call and express some kind of gratitude for his assistance. There weren't many people in the world who'd calmly take care of a person like that. It takes a special kind of heart.

She reached for the phone and punched in his number. By now, it had become part of her memory, but she still kept it written down, just in case. The phone rang once, and then again.

Detective Darrow's voice came over the line.

"Hello?"

"Hey, Blake. It's Alice."

"Oh hey, Alice! How are you feeling? Did you get the key I left?"

She twirled the phone cord like a middle school girl who was talking nervously with her crush. "Better now, and yep! I got it. Thanks so much for doing all that by the way. You really didn't need to —"

"Someone had to fix it properly. I really didn't mind."

"Not the lock — well yeah, that too! I mean, thanks for cleaning everything, and for doing the laundry. You really helped out a lot."

"It was no problem. A little puke never hurt anyone. Besides, it was my day off anyway. I get bored sitting at home doing nothing on the weekends."

"Well, maybe we could go out next Saturday?" she asked.

"Oh, really?" he said, with surprise in his voice. "That'd be nice. Where were you thinking of going?"

"Actually, I've been wanting to check out Kirt's Pub for a while. I've been hearing a lot about the place from the ladies at the salon, and it seems like several of the missing girls used to hang out there a lot."

"So, you're trying to investigate, then?" his tone became more serious and inquisitive.

"I guess you could put it like that. I just

figured that we could go in and ask a few questions. You know, to see if anyone can offer any information."

"Alice, these girls have been going missing for a few years now. Do you really think we haven't tried going in there multiple times by now? If anyone knows anything, they're not talking. Honestly, I think Kirt is getting tired of seeing my badge around the place."

"That's not what I meant. I'm sure you're all doing as much as you can, but the case has become kind of personal for me all of a sudden. If you don't want to go there with me, it's okay. I can go alone. The people might be more open to talking with a single gal anyway." She ended her statement with a chuckle, knowing that she had him cornered. She knew that if he had cared enough to hold her while she spewed vomit everywhere, then he definitely cared too much to let her go into that shady bar alone to ask people uncomfortable questions.

"Uh... dammit. Fine. What time should I get you?"

"Awesome! I'll be ready by 8. See you on Saturday!"

Click.

***

The work week went by quickly and uneventfully. Alice was very thankful for that. She sat in front of her vanity and did her makeup in the mirror. Detective Darrow was going to arrive in a matter of minutes, and she didn't have much time left to cake her face. She hurried to apply a light purple eye shadow, paired with a crimson lip. Despite the rush, it turned out very well after she had completed the look with a few passes of jet black mascara.

She teased a few of the curls that she'd placed in her hair earlier in the day and then sprayed them generously with hairspray. Small town bars always seemed strangely humid and damp, so she had to make sure that her hairstyle would last the entire evening. She felt around for Sarah's small yellow bow and placed it in her bangs. It added a fun vibe without making her look childish.

"Give me strength tonight."

With yellow pumps to match the bow, she threw on a tight black dress. It showed off her legs but still left enough to the imagination. It had been a while since she had gone out to a bar, and she knew that she was probably overdoing it. She didn't seem to care much about that though. She just wanted to remember what it was like to get dolled up again for something other than work.

There was a knock at the door, and she got up to answer it.

"All ready?" Detective Darrow asked.

The words slipped out before he had even taken a proper look at her. From head to toe, he stared at her for a moment, but not in a perverted way. He didn't look as if he was imagining anything. He just looked surprised and impressed, as if he were staring at the most expensive diamond in the world. His black monochrome outfit was much more casual than hers, but they still seemed to look good standing next to each other.

"M-hmm. Let's get going." She locked everything up, and they headed down the road.

***

Kirt's Pub was on the very edge of town, near the lake. It was just as humid there as Alice had expected that it would be. She could smell their greasy pizza baking from the kitchen area, and she tried to suppress the sudden hunger pangs. There were more important things to focus on.

"Back again, Darrow?" a voice piped up from behind the bar top.

"Nice to see you again, too, Kirt."

Kirt stood there, leaning slightly against the counter while he filled several pitchers. Light beer poured from one of the taps, and he tapped his fingers impatiently waiting for each one. He was a good-looking silver-haired man and didn't seem to suit the grungy environment that he was surrounded by.

"And, it's good to see you again, Alice. Strange company you keep." He looked at Detective Darrow disapprovingly, and then back to Alice. "Be careful around here though. It's a lot more wild on Saturdays than it is on the weeknights when you pick up your pizzas from the kitchen. Oh, the things I would give to have your genetics... I'd be as big as a house if I ate the shit that comes out of this place." He handed the pitchers off to a group of middle-aged couples and then gave his full attention to Alice and the detective. "Anyway, what do you want? Beer? Whiskey? A search warrant?" He asked as he looked at Detective Darrow disapprovingly.

"I guess we'll just have —"

"Beer it is," Kirt said, interrupting him. He thudded two glass cups onto the bar top and sat a frosty can of beer in each one. "This is better than what's on tap right now. Five bucks."

Detective Darrow placed five singles on the counter and reached for the glasses. He slid one next to him in front of Alice, and they both sat down in the ripped bar stools. The building was lit differently on the weekends, and people dance around drunkenly in a corner next to an outdated stereo. There were two waitresses roaming around, handing drinks off, and cleaning up different messes. Mostly, though, they sat on the laps of men, petting their sweaty heads, and pressing their lips against their salty necks. It became pretty obvious that these girls were into other forms of Customer Service.

"Is this what I think it is?" Alice whispered out of the corner of her mouth.

Detective Darrow nodded, confirming her suspicions. "I'm supposed to just look the other way. The chief comes here sometimes, so this place gets away with pretty much anything. Well, except for murder, of course."

"Well, I'd hope no one could get away with that."

"Yeah," he said while he twirled the base of his glass around on the counter. "Me too."

Kirt approached them once more and asked if they'd like another round. Both nodded, so he placed two more cans down.

"Hey, Kirt?" Alice asked.

"What is it, princess?" He wiped condensation and spilled liquor off of the waxy wood with a stained rag.

"What can you tell me about Jessica Roberts?"

"Well, what do you want to know about her? She was the first to disappear. I know that much."

"What was she like? Did she act differently before she went missing?"

Detective Darrow sipped his beer and listened to the exchange, pretending not to be interested, but he was bad at playing it cool. Kirt was in a good mood, though, so he didn't want to change that by being a constant reminder of the law.

"Jess was a lush if I ever saw one. She'd do anything for a drink, and I mean anything." Kirt paused to wave one of the waitresses over. "Brooke, you'd better put those chips down if you know what's good for you," he said, placing a hand on his hip. "You know you gained too much weight in jail from eating those nasty things every day."

The waitress laughed and imitated his

stance. "That's fine by me. I'm harder to kidnap this way."

They laughed together for a moment, and then Kirt turned his attention back to Alice.

"Where were we... Oh, yes. Jessica. Jess... She was nice. Now, don't get me wrong, but she was always sitting on the laps of anyone who'd buy her a drink. She used to work here, but I had to fire her for stealing a few bottles of vodka — and not the cheap well stuff, either."

"Did she steal often?"

He shook his head. "No, she was actually a pretty honest girl for the most part. The craving just got that bad, I guess. Even after I fired her, she never left, at least not until she went missing. It became pretty accepted around here that she probably just ran off with some random passerby who said he could supply her with all the cash and booze she'd want. I guess the whole town probably feels pretty stupid now."

"Is that what you thought at first, too? That she had just run off with someone?"

Kirt looked down and shook his head again. He looked back up with a serious expression on his face. "No, I knew better than that. There isn't a man in the whole world who's rich enough to keep that girl out of the bar. I knew that something sketchy definitely happened. I just didn't know what."

"When she was here the last time, was she with anyone?"

"Actually, yeah. She was hanging around with a few different guys. I didn't recognize any of them though, which isn't really all that unusual, to be honest. We get a lot of truckers stopping in for drinks. I didn't get to take a better look at them before they all left together, so I don't think I'd be even be able to identify them if they were standing right in front of me. It's been years anyway. My memory isn't that great, to begin with."

"I understand. Do you think you could tell me anything about the others though? Ashley or Tammy? I know Sarah didn't really come around here —"

"Actually," he interrupted. "Sarah stopped in for pizza sometimes, just like you. You're right though, she didn't come around late at night or on the weekends. Ashley — she did her fair share of partying, but nothing too crazy. And poor Tammy... She had a bad reputation as a lush, but I always saw her pouring her shots on the floor when no one else was looking. I think she just showed up for the male attention. Daddy issues, that one." He tapped his fingers on the bar top again and looked across the room. His serious expression changed into one of excitement and intrigue. "Now, you'll have to excuse me for a second. There's a really handsome gentleman by the stereo who needs a refill."

He winked and walked away faster than Alice could come up with any sort of reply.

She looked at Detective Darrow and shrugged. "Well, that's that, I guess."

"Did you hear what you wanted?" he asked, knowing that she wasn't satisfied.

She paused and stared off at the bottles of liquor for a moment. "I really don't know."

"How about we get out of here and go back to my place then. I can show you some of the things I've been trying to piece together about the case. Maybe some fresh eyes could help."

"Really? You can show me those things?"

"No, not really. Just don't tell anyone. Besides, some company would be a nice change."

"Well, what are we doing still wasting time in here then? Let's go!" she said with eagerness in her voice.

They stood up from their seats and left

a few more bills for Kirt. He nodded from across the room and waved. Just as the pair were nearing the door to leave, Benji walked inside and bumped into Alice. He recognized her and smiled, but then noticed Detective Darrow at her side. His expression changed to a scowl, and he passed by them quickly, suddenly acting as if they didn't even exist.

***

Detective Darrow's house was clean and organized, with very little decoration on the walls or tables. The lack of personal touch is what actually somehow ended up personalizing it just for him. It seemed fitting.

"Alright, you can sit here, and I'll bring a few things out of my office." He nodded over to a small table and chairs that were nestled beside the dining room window. "Can I get you something to drink?" he asked, motioning his hand to the kitchen.

"A drink would be nice, actually," she responded. "What do you have?"

"Well, there's soda, beer, tea. Actually, you know what? Just help yourself. Take whatever looks good, and grab one for me, too. I'll only be gone for a minute."

He headed down the hallway, and Alice walked up to the refrigerator.

Just like his decor, the contents of his fridge were pretty bare and uninteresting. He had all of the basics, but there were no signs that he ever cooked a real meal. Alice had no room to judge though. After all, she had basically been living off of pizza and fried rice for a month. She looked around at the drinks stacked on the bottom and decided on more beer. The cans were ice-cold in her hands and the frostiness numbed them slightly as she walked back to the dining room. She sat them down, one on each side, and relaxed into a sturdy wooden chair.

"I like your dining set," she called out, hoping that he could hear the compliment from his office.

Footsteps approached from the hallway, and Detective Darrow sat a few folders and stacks of papers down on the table in front of Alice. "Thanks. My dad actually made the set for me when I moved out for the first time."

"That's awesome. He did a really good job. Does he make furniture for a living, or is it more of a hobby? Maybe I could have him make something for me too some time."

"I really wish he could. He's been gone for almost a decade now. But, to answer your question, he made these sort of things as a hobby."

Alice looked down, embarrassed, and then looked up at Detective Darrow's face once more. "I'm sorry, I didn't —"

"Ah, don't be sorry. He was a good man, and of course, I miss him, but life has to go on. I try not to dwell on the fact that he's gone, and I try to focus on all of the fun times we had together while he was still here."

"That's a great way to look at things. My parents passed away before I could really form any memories. I don't know much about either of them, but I like to imagine that they were good people."

He nodded and looked through a few of the folders on the table. "If they were anything like you, I'm sure they would have been."

When he'd found the folder that he wanted to show her first, he opened it up and angled it so they could both see it. He scooted his chair closer to her and cracked open one of the beers. Once he'd taken a big gulp, Alice did the same.

"Okay, so, as I said, I haven't solved anything yet, but I definitely think that these cases are all linked. It doesn't seem like a coincidence at all, no matter what the others have been saying." He flipped through a couple of pages in the folder until he came upon a few photographs. He pulled them out and slid them directly in front of Alice. "These are a little graphic, so tell me if it gets to be too much for you. I don't want to freak you out or anything."

"Don't worry. I'm sure I'll be fine," she replied, reassuringly.

The first photo was a close-up of Jessica's head and face. Her skin was dark and discolored. The majority of it had rotted away, but some of it still remained intact. Brown hair barely clung to the bits on her scalp, but it had all been chopped very short. It looked as if someone had just grabbed handfuls of her hair and cut it off without any care or method in mind.

Alice remembered the dream. Sarah's hair had been cut carelessly too. Maybe the dream was more than that. Maybe it had been some sort of sign. She'd never been much of magical thinker before, but sometimes it could be hard to claim that things were only a coincidence. She continued examining the photo.

"See here?" Detective Darrow said, pointing to what was left of Jessica's nose. "The cartilage was mostly gone when we dug her up, but the bone looked like it had been bludgeoned or smashed somehow. That wasn't what killed her, but it's evidence of a struggle. Her ring and pinky fingers were both broken at the knuckles too. So she definitely fought back."

"That's just awful..." she said in a shocked tone. "If that's not what killed her, then how did she die?"

Detective Darrow looked down at the photo. "I think she was strangled. We can stop here if you want, or —" he paused.

"Maybe we should. It's just so terrible to think about how scared she must have been. Who could do this to someone?"

"I keep asking myself the same thing."

Ring Ring

"Hold on one second. I should probably take this." Detective Darrow got up and hurried to the phone. It didn't take much time for his expression to reach an entirely new level of seriousness. The fear in his eyes was a stark contrast to his usual happy and relaxed personality.

He lowered the phone and it clanked unsteadily as he hung it up. Slowly, he turned around and walked back to the table, his posture showing defeat. "I'm so sorry, but I have to go," he said with nervousness shaking around in his voice.

"Is everything okay? You look worried..." she asked, standing to her feet.

He shook his head and reached down to his folders to stack them neatly. "They think they found another body."

Chapter 12

"Hairspray"

The salon was gloomy, even for a Monday. The younger crowd was absent, either working or just hiding away safely in their homes. The older clients still showed up for their appointments though, fully prepared for their weekly washes and roller sets. The women either knew no fear or their need to gossip was just way too strong to keep them in the safety of their homes, in front of their TV sets.

Alice listened while a couple of the ladies discussed the latest events. It didn't take long before the two-person conversation had turned into something much larger. People gasped all around the room in between the short judgmental statements and observations. Everyone had an opinion, and a lot of them even had the same opinions, but their desire to repeat them over and over in different ways out-weighed the redundancy for the most part.

"My niece, the one who's married to the chief's brother," a woman said, her voice much louder than the others. "Well, she said that the bones probably belonged to Tammy Thomas. I don't know how they'd confirm something like that though. She said that someone had tried to burn them."

"Poor Tammy," another woman gasped. "She was actually pretty sweet. Has anyone heard about how she might have died?" The woman's eyes scanned the room, and for a few seconds, there was silence.

The brief silence was broken by the hanging bell that rattled against the entrance door. Betty walked in and looked around sheepishly. Her hair was tangled and greasy looking. It looked as if she had just woken up. She sat down in the waiting area, and her hands reached over to the table next to her for one of the outdated magazines. Once it was in her grip, she flipped through the pages, avoiding eye contact.

"Good morning Betty," Edna's voice sang out toward her. "The usual?"

Betty looked up for a brief moment to nod and add a comment. "A trim, too, if that's okay."

"Of course it is. I'll put you with Alice once she's done with Annie."

Alice piped up quickly and warmly. "We're actually all done... Just one more pass of the hairspray, and..." She sat the big metal can on the counter. It clanked loudly as if it were nearly empty. "Voila! There we go."

Annie smiled and patted her hair appreciatively before setting a dollar down for a tip. She got up from the styling chair quickly and sat back down in the waiting area so she could still participate in the conversations.

The women continued chattering about the bones that had been found in the woods near the lake. The wooded area, land, and water, sat on the very edge of town. Betty and a handful of other people in the community were able to consider it as their backyard. There was no fencing on their properties. There was nothing keeping any of them from walking down to dip their toes into the murky water. Their homes had once been envied by many of the people in town, but now they were just another part of the nightmare that had enveloped Wintersburg. No one wanted any part of the lake anymore.

Betty's expression never changed during the discussion though, even when asked about the crime scene. It was as if she was in a content little daze, completely oblivious to the severity of the situation. Alice didn't mind. It was much better than seeing her drunk and acting erratically as she had done previously. Since that strange April night, Betty had only appeared in the salon two other times, about half as much as she typically would have shown up to have her hair styled.

Alice didn't judge much though. She knew what it was like for people to have things held against them, and she didn't think it was right to do that to others. She knew how deeply teasing could hurt a person. She knew how much something as simple as a cruel stare could haunt a person for years, or even for a lifetime. Even though Alice had blossomed into an attractive young woman, her younger years had been difficult at times. Like many preteens, she had an awkward phase. Her phase just happened to last a few years longer than the other girls' phases, so she had to deal with the pain of sticking out for quite a bit longer than her peers. When she was only eleven, the words of one girl in particular — a girl whose full name had completely dissolved out of her mind — had hurt her more than any of the others before. They etched themselves in the reflection of every mirror that she passed by from then on.

"No matter how hard you try to hide, everyone can still see how ugly you are."

The words had haunted Alice like a ghost for twelve whole years. Over time, she learned to paint her face and tease her hair. She hid behind her mask like that same scared eleven-year-old girl had hidden behind her stacks of books and long stringy hair. But to everyone else, Alice appeared confident and stylish. She was the city girl with big dreams and a career. No one saw that the makeup was holding her fragile face together like glue, or that one false move of a mascara wand was enough to crack the water-filled porcelain around her eyes. No one saw Alice as Alice. She was just pretty.

***

Alice walked with Betty over to the

shampoo bowl and politely instructed her to sit down, as was usual. She placed a towel into the groove of the bowl for Betty to rest her thin neck onto. It was much more comfortable to do that than to let her visible spine grind against the cold hard porcelain while she was being shampooed. The little things were actually very important.

She turned the water on, and lifted the hose, angling it toward the drain. It always took just a little too long for things to heat up, but it gave Alice time to look for any gray hairs or split ends that might need to be addressed. Her eyes noticed little specks of something along the ends of Betty's short hair.

"It's probably just mud or something," she thought, as she took notice of the amount of grease that had accumulated near Betty's scalp this time. *"She hasn't been in for a wash in a while."*

The water finally reached a reasonable temperature, so she pointed the hose over Betty's dirty hair. Her hands finger-combed through the ends while she tried to break up the little chunks as carefully as possible, avoiding hurting Betty's tender scalp. Fortunately, the grime had started to dissolve rather quickly. Alice looked into the bowl and noticed that the water was changing colors as it traveled down the strands of hair. Normally, it would have turned more of a brownish tint from the hair treatments and various rinses, but not this time.

The water was red.

Images flashed through Alice's mind, taking her back to the dream that she'd had of Sarah. She saw Sarah's frightened eyes, begging her for help. She felt her ice-cold breath against her skin again. She saw the blood, and the clumps of shorn dark hair on the floor, with coagulation encompassing them, holding each of the strands together like little bouquets of dead roses.

She froze in place, and the water continued to pour out over Betty's hair.

"Alice, are you okay?" Edna's voice broke through the silent flashback as she walked toward the shampoo bowl. "Oh, Betty, I see you've been painting again," she said as she looked down at the water.

Edna walked to the opposite side of the bowl and gently took the hose from Alice's hand. She turned the water off temporarily and ran a few pumps of shampoo through Betty's hair. The red paint bubbled and turned into cotton-candy-pink suds as she worked it through her scalp and ends. She lifted her eyes to Alice's and smiled reassuringly. Her hand reached for the nozzle and she turned the hose on once more to rinse the shampoo out.

"It's okay," she mouthed out silently. Edna was very aware of the stress than Alice had been under. The entire town was experiencing it, after all. She lifted Betty's head and dried everything with a towel before offering one final thought. "Oh, Betty. I almost forgot to ask if you were going to be setting up a booth for the fundraiser tonight."

"Yeah, I'll be in the spare lot next to Medley's. That's where I was told to set my stand up, anyway. I guess the mayor wants all of the food in one location this time. I'm guessing he didn't like having to walk around so much at the City-wide Yard Sale last summer." Her eyes closed for a moment as if she were trying to recall something. She rubbed the tension from her brow and lifted a finger excitedly to Edna. Her entire mood changed from what could be compared to catatonic bliss to more of an enthusiastic salesperson. "I've been trying out a few new barbecue sauces too. I'm going to sell a mild and a hot. I think they'll go over really well. Make sure to stop by, and I'll give you extra."

Edna smiled appreciatively. "I'm sure everyone will love them. And I'll be sure to find you to try them out if I get a chance to walk around."

"Well, I hope you can. I have good feelings about this batch. The pigs have been nice and fat this year. The pork should be really sweet."

Edna smiled warmly and then raised her eyes to Alice. She winked and gave her a thumbs-up before walking away. The diversion had helped Alice more than she probably even realized.

Alice took over again and walked Betty back to the styling chair. She felt a bit embarrassed for her reaction to the paint but was thankful for Edna's help. It felt good to listen to polite conversation, and it seemed to have calmed her down quite a lot.

"Alright, here you go, Betty. Let's get you all taken care of."

"You know — I've been thinking," Betty uttered softly as she plopped herself into the seat. "Would you be willing to come to my place to do my hair from now on?"

Alice, cutting-comb in hand, stared at her with confusion for a moment. She wasn't sure how to respond to the suggestion. Edna hadn't specifically told her not to style clients in their homes, but it was basic etiquette to keep the money in the salon.

"I'd still pay you, of course, even a little more actually. You can even take some pork home if you'd like. I have way too much of it in the deep freezer right now — more than I could even dream to sell. I just haven't been feeling great lately, and it would be nice to have one less thing to worry about." Betty stopped speaking for a moment to stare at Alice's reflection in the mirror.

Alice didn't seem to be against the idea, but she still appeared to be unsure.

Betty offered more words to help convince her of the idea. "It's just that, you know, the gossip around can be a little too much for me, and now with that second body showing up, I just can't —"

"Actually, I totally understand, Betty. To be completely honest, I'm getting tired of hearing all of these crazy rumors too. I can only imagine how much harder it is for you." She realized that Betty probably needed the help more than the salon needed the small cost of a roller set. She could always put the money in the drawer anyway. Edna would understand.

Betty smiled into the mirror, appearing happier than she had been in a long time. It was as if a significant weight had been immediately lifted from her chest, and she was suddenly able to breathe deeply again. Since there weren't any other salons in town, she'd been suffering through the whispers and judgmental glances of her neighbors for months, simply to maintain some sort of a shred of normalcy with her appearance. That month had been the most difficult, especially since Roger had been policing her wine intake. Her newly disheveled state was evidence of her inability to cope well with a sober mind.

"Thank you. Thanks so much, Alice," she said with more life in her voice. "I'm always home on Tuesdays. Since the salon closes at 7, do you think you could come by after those shifts?"

Alice nodded. "That sounds good to me. I'll just need a little time to gather my things, so I should be there by 7:30 each Tuesday."

"Wonderful. I really can't even tell you how much I appreciate this."

"Don't worry about it. Now, let's get your hair trimmed so you can get out of here." Alice parted Betty's hair into sections and clipped each one out of the way. She placed a hair-cutting cape across her torso and tied a paper strip around her neck to provide an extra layer of defense against the hair clippings.

"Hold on one second. I almost forgot something," Betty said. She lifted her hands up behind her head and fumbled around under the paper strip. After a few seconds, she produced a short necklace and sat it onto the counter in front of the mirror. It sparkled uncontrollably beneath the fluorescent salon lights, glittering like thousands of fireflies. Among the crystals that lined the chain, a light lavender pendant sparkled with a little more modesty.

"I can't risk having that get nicked by scissors," she said while readjusting her weight. "Okay, just an inch all over, at the most. Oh, and could you cut around the ears too? Those pesky hairs keep going wild when I wear my reading glasses."

Alice stared at the necklace, her gaze resembling a deer frozen from fear in the street. Between Betty's newly social personality, the red sink water, and now this, she was absolutely overwhelmed.

"Yeah, sure..." she said, her voice trailing off as if she hadn't even listened to the request. "Where did you get this necklace?"

"Oh, this?" she said, pointing at the roped pile of sparkles. "It was my daughter, Sarah's. I've been wearing it a lot lately."

***

The fundraiser seemed to be going well when Alice arrived. Medley's parking lot, the spare lot, and the plot of bare land next to it — about an acre of grass — were filled with people and tables. It was as if the whole town felt safe enough to leave their homes temporarily to gather around for raffles and homemade pies. Kids ran around with sticky hands and powdered sugar on their faces, while the adults held onto cold beer bottles and wiped spilled barbecue sauce onto their jeans. The sweet smoky smell of pulled pork filled the air, and even Alice had been tempted to try a bite or two. She followed her nose all the way across the lot and found the food stands.

As soon as her eyes saw Betty and her multiple crock pots, she felt a hand rest gently onto her shoulder. She turned around to see who it had belonged to.

"Well, if it isn't Blake Darrow," she said, in a teasing tone. "Are you here to show your support?"

"Damn right, I am. I'll buy as many funnel cakes as it takes to build a new playground. The other one is so rusty, I'm afraid the slides are going to disintegrate beneath someone one day. Can you imagine the paperwork for that?" He laughed and licked the powdered sugar from his fingertips.

"Sugar, huh? Are you sure the playground isn't for you?"

"Oh come on, Alice. You can't honestly say that this doesn't look absolutely amazing." He held his paper plate closer to her face and tilted it so she could see the funnel cake better. The powdered sugar moved around as the light breeze hit it, causing it to puff up into the air like smoke. "This is the best thing here. I swear."

"I can't lie. It looks pretty good. I was thinking about trying Betty's pork though. I keep hearing people talk about it, so it has to be pretty special, right?" She looked over toward the stand again and watched as Betty's brother, Will, delicately stacked the Wonderbread buns neatly beside one of the crockpots. She wondered if he was always so gentle.

"Just try a bite first, and see if you still want a sandwich. If you do, it's my treat. If not, you're buying us another one of these to split."

Alice sighed, pretending to be annoyed with his suggestion, but immediately smiled afterward. She reached her hand out for the fork, but Detective Darrow fed her a piece, himself. She chewed it up, trying not to laugh from the surprise. Powdered sugar dusted her lips, and she lifted her hands to shield her face as she licked it away.

"It's good, huh?" he asked, grinning with confidence. "Want another bite?"

"Dammit. It really is good," she said, wiping her mouth the rest of the way with her wrist. "Fine. You win. I'll get us another one."

"I knew it!" he exclaimed, seeming more like a child than a police officer.

Alice shook her head and dug around in her purse for her wallet. She really enjoyed seeing Detective Darrow let loose like this. It was as if he became a completely different person without his uniform on. While she still enjoyed being around him when he was working, she also liked seeing his goofy more-human side. He seemed vulnerable with sugar on his shirt where his badge would normally rest, and it made her feel more comfortable standing so closely to him. He wasn't Detective Darrow with vanilla on his breath — he was just Blake.

They headed toward the funnel cake stand and the scent of grease hit Alice's nose. These sort of places always smelled so dirty, but so delicious at the same time. She bit her bottom lip as the smell grew stronger, anticipating more sugary goodness.

"Almost there," she said, turning her head to see if Detective Darrow was as excited as she was. After all, this had been his idea, technically.

"Oh," he said, staring off in the other direction. He stopped walking. "Looks like Sheriff Gray decided to stop by."

"Sheriff Gray? What's so bad about him?" she asked, curious as to what he could have done to deserve such a reaction.

"Well, there's nothing wrong with him. He's a good guy, I guess — a good sheriff. I just didn't want my toes to be stepped on this early, you know? With the county stepping in to look into the case, my hands are a little more tied than before. They're going to expect me and the guys to follow their rules now."

"Oh, well, it's good to have some help though, don't you think? The more eyes looking into things, the better."

Detective Darrow shook his head. "They're going to rush it. I guarantee it. Something's going to be missed or overlooked, just so they can go around with proud looks on their faces. All they care about is telling everyone that they saved the day. The wrong people have been arrested for things like this before if you want my honest opinion."

"Try to stay optimistic. I'm sure they'll do fine." Alice said reassuringly. She had confidence that more resources meant better results. In her mind, Detective Darrow just wanted to solve things by himself and was projecting his insecurities. "Just do your thing and answer to him later."

"That's the plan."

Sheriff Gray nodded and approached them. He held a paper plate with two pulled pork sandwiches and a generous pile of coleslaw on it. There was confidence in the way he walked, almost intimidating in a way. While barbecue sauce dripped all over everyone else's hands, he managed to stay clean by cutting into his sandwich with the side of a plastic fork. He ate it as gracefully and emotionlessly as it could be eaten in such a setting.

"Darrow," he said, tilting his head down before turning it to Alice. "Ma'am." He took another bite from his fork and chewed it slowly, smashing most of it into a small mound in his cheek.

"Sheriff," Detective Darrow replied, tilting his head in the same way. "I didn't think you'd be wandering around here today."

"I didn't either, but I thought it'd be a good chance to talk with some of the townsfolk to see if anyone has anything they'd like to say. People tend to open up to new faces more quickly than the ones they have to see every day." He cut into one of his sandwiches again.

"Hopefully you find what you're looking for. As for the two of us, we're on the hunt for another funnel cake. It was good to see you, Sheriff. I'm sure I'll be seeing you around a lot more."

"Same to you, detective. Enjoy yourselves."

The men nodded in unison and turned away from each other. Alice wondered if she had just witnessed the equivalent of a male catfight, but resisted asking any more questions about the topic. She had been enjoying Blake's sugar-coated personality up until then and wanted to savor it for as long as she could. There was no reason to allow such a simple encounter to leave a bad taste in their mouths.

Chapter 13

"Girls Just Want To Have Fun"

The red light on the answering machine blinked at Alice when she entered the kitchen. She'd been terrible about checking her messages ever since moving to Wintersburg, but she felt like she might as well sit and finally listen to them. Her body was tired, and her mind was even more exhausted. The light vanished from the machine as soon as she pressed the button. Slowly, she sank down against the wall, letting her bottom hit the floor. With her knees pressed up to her chest, she inhaled deeply, freeing her mind of all other distractions.

There were a few annoying messages from telemarketers at first — some trying to sell her on the latest Get-Slim-Quick scheme, others trying to convince her to join in on the newest and very obvious pyramid scheme. Edna had even called to see if she needed anything. After a quick message from Tiffany, asking if she had any free time for a girl's night out, she heard Detective Darrow's deep voice playing back.

"Hey, Alice. It's Blake. There's a little bit of news about Jessica that you might be interested in hearing. Anyway, give me a call back whenever you get this. Buh-bye."

Click.

Alice stood up quickly and grabbed the phone. The cord was in knots as usual, but instead of taking the time to un-twirl them, she just stood very close to the wall, practically allowing her hair to tangle in with the mess as well. Detective Darrow's phone number was hammered like a nail into her memory, and she pushed the seven digits without even thinking.

The phone rang several times before it went to his voicemail.

"You've reached Blake Darrow. I'm unable to answer the phone right now, but if you leave me your name, number, and the reason you're calling, I'll get back to you as soon as I can. Have a good day."

"How... formal," she thought, humorously. *"The harder he tries to be serious, the goofier he comes across."*

The line beeped, and she hung the phone up instead of leaving a message. She figured that he was probably just busy with work, and he'd end up calling her back again when he was free anyway. There wasn't really a need to go back and forth leaving each other vague messages every few hours.

She slumped back down to the floor and resumed her exhausted looking position. The stress of the day coursed through her body like resistant bacteria, causing her thoughts to go septic. She thought of Betty, and then she thought of the necklace.

"Why had Betty been wearing it? That's not something that Sarah would just leave behind. She wore it in every single picture that I came across so far. It was practically a part of her. Dead or alive, shouldn't she still be wearing it?"

Thoughts conflicted in her head. Betty, while strange and unstable, didn't seem like a violent woman though. Surely, she wasn't the type to murder anyone. She didn't seem like a thief either. After all, she'd immediately admitted that it was Sarah's necklace when Alice had asked about it.

"Maybe Sarah really did forget it? Maybe she just gave it to her mom as a parting gift or something?"

It still wasn't adding up, but it also wasn't raising enough flags for her to dwell on the topic — at least, not at the moment. Alice yawned and rested her head heavily onto her arms that had been crisscrossed over her knees. As soon as the tense air left her lungs, someone knocked excitedly on the front door.

She jumped up, startled. *"Who on earth would be here right now?* The sun's already gone down."

She looked at the time on the clock before making her way out of the kitchen.

8:47

"Ugh," she said out loud as her feet traveled into the living room. She reached for the door handle and opened it without checking the window first. She almost always looked to see who was outside before answering, but she had been a little absent-minded at that moment. The door swung open and bright flaming hair greeted her from the porch.

"Tiff! What are you doing here?" she asked, excitedly.

"Hey, you didn't call me back, jerk." She said, laughing at her own statement as she punched Alice lightly against the shoulder. She stepped forward.

Alice was used to having Tiffany make herself right at home, so she just moved out of the way. There was no need to formally invite her inside.

Tiffany waltzed over to the refrigerator and looked inside it with a disapproving expression on her face. She closed the door and turned back to Alice. "I'm starving. Want me to get a pizza for us?" she asked, already heading toward the phone.

"I don't think I have a choice, do I?

Tiffany shook her head and dialed Kirt's Pub. She almost immediately started placing an order. "Yeah, I'll just have a large pizza with extra cheese. M-hmm. For pick up." There was a brief pause, and then she resumed talking. "Twenty minutes? Okay. I'll be there then!"

She hung up the phone and turned to Alice again. "Let's hop in my car. We'll grab some sodas from Medley's on the way."

"Okay, I have to find my purse real quick."

"My treat. Just leave it here." Tiffany grabbed Alice's keys from the counter and headed back toward the front door.

Alice followed behind and waited while she locked it for them. This was all starting to become a weekly routine, and she actually enjoyed the assertive company. It kept her out of her head. It kept her living.

Tiffany, with her poor manners and carefree spirit, welcomed Alice into her life like a small-town pub welcomes the same old beer-loving faces into its doors. Sure, both were somewhat brash at times, but they always knew what you needed at that moment — whether it was a friend, a shoulder to lean on, or just a familiar environment to be around. She was always there for Alice when she needed someone or something. She was a true friend — something that Alice had been really missing in her life for a long time.

***

Kirt's Pub was loud and rowdy, especially for a weeknight. Pitchers of beer were sitting carelessly on top of the edges of both of the pool tables, practically begging to be knocked over by any one of the sweat-covered people who had been sloppily smashing into each other like wet balls of dough. The air smelled like a mixture of old draft beer and the musty onion-tinged stench of either body odor or onion rings. It was difficult to tell the difference. Alice's eyes became irritated, and they watered as she and Tiffany cut through the crowd.

They sat down next to each other in a pair of stools. Fortunately, there were several seats available since the crowd mostly seemed to prefer dancing and swaying into one another at that moment. The air was slightly less funky smelling from where they were seated, but it was still ridiculously damp. That was to be expected though.

"What can I get for you ladies," Kirt's voice said, seeming to appear almost out of nowhere. "We're all out of cans, so it's just bottles or draft tonight." He shifted his weight onto one of his hips and dabbed at his forehead with the rag that he'd been using to wipe down the bar-top. Tiny beads of sweat glistened across his skin, reflecting the various colored light bulbs all around, causing him to slightly resemble the Lite-Brite toy that Alice had wanted when she was younger.

"That's fine," Alice said. "We're just here to pick up a pizza tonight."

"Actually, hold on a second." Tiffany turned to Alice and had excitement written all over her face. She twirled her hair in her fingers as if she was trying to curl each of the little pieces with the heat from her hands. "What if we just ate here? We can order a few beers and let loose a little."

"So, what was the point of picking up sodas on the way over then?" Alice asked, a little confused by the sudden change in plans.

"It's not like they'll go bad or something. I'm sure we'll want to drink them eventually. Does that stuff even expire anyway?"

Alice stretched her arms out in front of her and tapped on the bar-top for a moment. She inhaled deeply and let out a long sigh of defeat. "Fine. You're right. I guess it wouldn't hurt us to have a little fun..."

"That's the spirit!" Tiffany hollered back while clapping enthusiastically.

"...As long as I'm home before midnight. I still have to work in the morning," Alice finished her reply.

"We have a deal then. I have to open tomorrow at the diner too, so I can't be out all night anyway."

The pair turned back to face Kirt. He was rolling his eyes in the direction of a few drunken mid-fifties women who had been trying to turn a support beam into a stripper pole. They were succeeding. "What'll it be, girls? Are you eating here, or what?" he asked.

"We'll eat here, I guess," Alice said. "And we'll take a pitcher of whatever light beer you have on tap."

"Mm-hmm, okay. I'll be right back." He waltzed into the kitchen, grabbed the food, and turned back around almost as quickly as he had left. The large cardboard box of pizza rested on top of his palm, and he presented it in front of them as if it were much higher quality than it actually had been. He sat a few paper plates and napkins down next to the box and filled a pitcher.

"Here you go. Let me know if you need anything else," he said as he sat the beer down, along with a couple of plastic cups.

"Thanks, Kirt. It looks delicious!"

Tiffany nodded at Alice's remark and smiled very appreciatively while she lifted a huge cheesy slice to her mouth. Grease dripped down her hand and onto her wrist, but she didn't seem very bothered by the messiness. She blotted it all away with little care or strategy between slices.

Alice's appetite was much more suppressed than Tiffany's had been that night. She took significantly smaller, fewer bites from her portion, and focused the majority of her attention on the beer instead. Even though she was supposed to be having a carefree fun time, she couldn't help but to reflect repeatedly on all of the things that had been happening since she moved to that town. She wasn't bitter. She was just overwhelmed, tired, and confused. Just like the multiple times she'd spent thinking about the town's events before, she couldn't help but to feel as if she were actually the bad omen. While the women had all gone missing before she'd ever even thought to show up in town, none of the bodies had been found until her arrival. People were still in a state of blissful denial until the gruesome truth had been dug up from those shallow graves.

Alice thought of the four women. Two were still in or on the earth somewhere, just waiting to be found. And, there were two others who had become nothing more than the small stacks of bones that were being passed back and forth between the hands of crime experts. After spending their entire lives dreaming, growing, and loving, the women had been left to rot alone in the mud that they'd once spent their childhood summers playing in. Only now, their mothers weren't able to rinse the grime away and tuck them into bed. They could only cry at the loss of life as they lifted dusty white sheets across the adult-sized skulls that had once formed so carefully in their wombs. There were no beds waiting for their daughters — just cold evidence cabinets and flower-adorned graves.

"Um, are you okay, Alice?" Tiffany asked, chewing on the end of a pizza crust. "You're more quiet than usual tonight."

"Yeah, I'm fine. I've just been a little distracted, I guess."

Alice swirled the plastic cup of beer around in her hand as if it were a glass of fine wine. She stared into the bubbles, getting lost momentarily in the beautiful light amber color. It reminded her of her grandmother's eyes. She could almost see them staring back at her from the depths of the drink.

"Yeah, I can see that..." Tiffany said, grabbing her by the hand as she hopped off of the bar stool. She yanked playfully at Alice's arm and started to drag her toward the makeshift dance floor. "Come on. Let's stop sitting around." She said to Alice. Then she nodded to Kirt, and shouted, "Two shots of whiskey, my man. Two each, I mean!"

A smile spread across his face as if he were surprised by the situation unfolding in front of him.

Alice, while not shy, was fairly reserved when it came to the bar. She didn't really dance or mingle with anyone during the times that she'd visited before. It had mainly just been a local pizza place in her mind.

Kirt stared on, excitedly. He occasionally allowed his eyes to wander over to the handsome regular who was chugging beers like some sort of a frat boy, admiring his strong jaw as he guzzled. Mostly, though, he kept his attention on Alice and Tiffany, waiting for something amusing to happen.

The girls danced around, slowly becoming less and less tense in their movements as the shots medicated their inhibitions. They had needed a night like this — a night without worry, a night without fear.

Chapter 14

"Tainted Love"

Detective Darrow got dressed for the day, and slid on a pair of comfortable shoes. He had decided to walk over to Alice's house to talk to her in person about the voicemail that he'd left for her on the answering machine the day before. He wondered if she hadn't been easy to reach lately, or if he'd actually been the busy one. With such chaos going on in the town, he'd been heavily focused on trying to find a suspect, a motive, or a link of some kind, any kind. The Clay County Sheriff's deputies were already in town, canoeing across the lake, looking for any and every speck of evidence that they could find around the water.

He didn't trust the deputies much more than he trusted whoever was out there killing people. He felt like the case needed to be handled quietly, and with much less of a scene, but his hands were tied. Since the new bones had been found, this was no longer a case for the Wintersburg police to handle alone. Their station needed the county's resources.

Detective Darrow knocked on Alice's door and paced back and forth while waiting, just as usual.

"Coming! Just a second!" her voice called out to him.

He saw her head peek through the blinds in the living room, and then the doorknob rattled for a brief moment.

"Blake! I've been meaning to call you back again. I tried to call yesterday, but you didn't answer. I figured that you were working or something." She shifted around for a moment, debating on whether to invite him inside or not. Her hair was up in a towel, freshly washed, and she felt a little insecure about her bare face. After all, he had just interrupted her shower, so she was in her most natural state. As soon as she had heard someone knocking at the door, she'd turned the water off and threw on the nearest bathrobe. This definitely didn't seem like a good time for her to be having any company, at least, not in her mind.

Detective Darrow stared at her for a few seconds. Sure, he'd always thought that she was a pretty girl, but she seemed even more beautiful without all of the usual glitz and glam. He wondered why she even bothered painting her face with all of those colorful eye shadows and lipsticks each morning. He saw beauty in her bare face — something that was almost a sin to cover up. His eyes wandered to her bare lips, and he admired their soft tones.

"Uh, I'm sorry," he said, without even thinking about his words or whether he even needed to apologize for something in the first place. "You're right. I've been tied up at work a lot this week." He lifted his wrist and glanced quickly at his thick black watch. It was a little too stylish for his casual outfit, but it was the only one he owned that hadn't been completely ruined yet. "I don't have a lot of time right now to talk about this, but I wanted to let you in on some things — if you're interested, I mean."

"Yeah, I'd like that a lot. Do you want to come in, or...?" she asked, her voice trailing off as she pointed behind her.

"I wish I could, but I can't risk getting too comfortable and losing any more time. Actually, I have to meet someone at the diner in about twenty more minutes."

"Oh, okay," she replied, confused and curious. "Well then, what's going on?" She knew that it was odd for Detective Darrow to be on-duty while in plain clothes, but she figured that he'd provide an explanation without any further prodding. She was right.

"When I called you, I had just heard that one of the server's from Kirt's Pub had been pulled into a car while she was leaving work. At the time, we had been interviewing her at the station and thought that we had a pretty good description of the guy. She said that the man was bald, middle-aged, and was driving an old beat-up silver truck. She also seemed to fit the type of the other girls enough — brunette, a little wild, so we thought that this was going to lead us right to him."

Alice gasped at the idea of another girl possibly being taken and killed somewhere. She noticed that Detective Darrow was pushing his short dark hair back and away from his forehead — something that he often did when he was uncomfortable or lost in thought. "So, what happened then? Is she okay? Do you know who the guy is?" she asked, flustered from the pause.

"Well, the problem is..." he mumbled while readjusting his posture to look more confident and less fidgety. "She made the whole thing up."

"What?" Alice interrupted. "Why in the world would anyone make something like that up?"

"That's what we were all asking ourselves too. Sheriff Gray and his deputies were having a pretty big laugh at our expense when they heard about the whole thing. You see, she finally gave us an explanation after we'd threatened her with more jail time. I'm sure you remember the girl, actually. She's the one that Kirt was yelling at about the chips when we went in there together. Brooke... She's not a new face around the station — that's for sure." He chuckled a little at that thought but quickly composed himself again when Alice nodded. "After some convincing, she explained that she had really been cheating on her boyfriend, Eric, that night with some random guy from the bar. I guess she had been gone for the entire evening. She told us that she had passed out and needed a little alibi. She's not the brightest girl, so she thought it would be a great idea to just fake a kidnapping. She'd even gone as far as to describe the room that the man had kept her in and everything. Really sick stuff."

Alice was confused but very interested. "So, why didn't she just tell her boyfriend that she'd gone to a friend's house for the night? It seems like that would have caused a lot less trouble than getting the cops involved. I mean, what did she think was going to happen?"

Detective Darrow shook his head and grinned. He'd been just as entertained while this whole situation was happening, despite the embarrassment, and he still held onto a bit of that amusement. "Eric had already called all of her friends to see if she was with any of them. I guess no one wanted to get involved, so they all threw her under the bus to deal with the situation herself. From my understanding, this wasn't the first time she'd stayed out all night with another man. Eric actually pieced everything together before we even could."

"How'd he find out?" she said, leaning in a little closer as if her ears would be able to catch the words faster that way.

"Kirt," he said, laughing as he spoke the name. "Kirt told him everything that he'd seen from start to finish when he had been calling around looking for her that night. The second that Eric had heard that Brooke was at the police station saying that she'd been forced into some man's truck, he came in and let us know that she was lying."

"Oh my God, that is absolutely insane!" her voice burst out with excitement. She was confused by Detective Darrow's sudden interest in gossip, but she definitely wasn't intending on complaining about it. This was the most entertaining thing she'd heard in a while. She felt like she was listening in on one of those wild day-time talk shows, where everyone was sleeping around with each other's partners. She loved it.

"Wait a minute. It gets even crazier," he said, wiping the sweat from the back of his neck. He didn't do well in the heat. "They started arguing really loud right in the station, to the point that an officer had to step in to remove Brooke from the room. While she was being restrained, Eric ended up admitting that she hadn't been the only person cheating in the relationship. He had been cheating on her for a long time too. Anyway, I know we're both rushed so I'll just get to the point of this whole thing."

Alice waited eagerly for more words to leave his lips. She was still confused about where he was going with this whole story, and why it was so important to explain during such a time crunch, but she figured that it must have been significant in some way. Her heart fluttered painfully when she heard the explanation as if it were being squeezed by someone's hand.

"Eric had been cheating on her with Jessica Roberts a few years ago."

Alice immediately thought of Tiffany, and how frightened she seemed underneath her tough exterior after finding Jessica's body. "Do — do you think he had something to do with —" she asked, practically choking on her words.

"I really don't think so, but I've been surprised before. But, I actually have to get out of here now. He's the person I'm meeting up with."

Alice nodded and looked into Detective Darrow's eyes. She was suddenly very nervous for him. "Please be safe... and keep in touch. You can't just tell me all of this and then leave me hanging, okay?"

"Don't worry," he said, resting his hands gently across her robe-covered shoulders. "Everything will be fine, and I'll fill you in on the details later. I'd just like to interview Eric before Sheriff Gray gets to him. Things like this need to be looked into on a personal level. I'm going to try to talk to him man to man instead of man to monster. For all we know, he's innocent. It's best to treat him like he is for now. Anyway, I just want you to worry about being cautious. I'll give you a call later." He stepped back and waved, coyly. Not only was he short on time, but he was also only seconds away from showing more affection than what was appropriate. He collected himself and hopped into his car.

***

The diner was fairly empty. The early morning rush had already calmed down, and lunch was still a few hours away. Detective Darrow scanned the tables, looking for a familiar face. As he reached the far corner of the restaurant, he saw Eric sitting in a booth alone, staring down at the menu in front of him. The man kept his back to the entrance, but he was still easy to identify due to the brown leather jacket and a ball cap that he always wore, regardless of the weather. Detective Darrow had assumed that there was something he was hiding underneath the sleeves — either tattoos or something else he didn't want anyone to know about.

He sat down across from Eric and gave a friendly nod. Eric pushed the menu toward him and smiled slightly in return. The man was visibly uncomfortable and scared, but Detective Darrow had no intentions of intimidating him any further.

Footsteps approached the pair but stopped before they reached the table.

Tiffany gasped slightly, but she then continued walking. *"What is Darrow doing with that guy?"* she wondered, recognizing the man as the one who had frightened her with his weird mannerisms back in April. She cleared her throat, trying to steady the surprise in her voice, and pulled out a pen and notepad.

"What can I get for you this morning?" she asked, trying not to make eye contact.

"Hey, Tiffany. How's your day going so far?" Detective Darrow interjected.

"Um, well, it's goin' I guess. Can I get some coffee for you?"

"Actually," he looked over to Eric to see if he had any suggestions. He didn't. "Just bring us out a fresh pot of the strong stuff, and a stack of creamers, if you could."

She nodded and stared at the pad of paper in her hand. "Anything to eat?" she asked.

Eric shook his head.

"I think we'll be fine with just the coffee, Tiff, but thanks." Detective Darrow replied for both of them.

"Alright. I'll be back shortly."

Tiffany walked away and made a new pot of coffee. She added an extra scoop of coffee grounds into the filter to make sure it was nice and strong. After scooping several little creamers into her apron, she took it all over to the table, along with two mugs. "Let me know if you need anything else. The place is pretty empty, so feel free to yell if you can't see me."

"Sounds like a plan," Detective Darrow replied.

Tiffany walked over to the same table that she had hidden behind the first time Eric had shown up. Just as she had done before, she pretended to clean it by wiping the same spot over and over again. She felt guilty for spying last time, but she was even more interested now than she had been before. This definitely didn't seem like the type of company that Detective Darrow would typically keep, but he was acting casually, and even having coffee with the guy like they were old pals.

She watched as they talked for a while. Eric eventually reached into his jacket. He pulled out the same folded piece of paper that he had been staring at the last time Tiffany had been spying on him. She squinted to see what it said as he passed it over to Detective Darrow.

"Tiff," a voice came from behind her. "I

need your help cleaning a mess in the kitchen."

"Ugh. Fine. I didn't want to know anything anyway," she mumbled under her breath as she followed her coworker into the back. She turned around one more time before continuing on, defeatedly. "Dammit." she thought.

Detective Darrow delicately grabbed the paper from Eric.

"Missing"

It was the original flyer that used to hang outside of Medley's for Jessica before the other names and faces were added to the list. Eric's tough exterior suddenly cracked, and a few tears welled in his eyes.

"It's the only picture I have of her," he said with a strained voice. "I keep it with me all the time."

"I understand," Detective Darrow replied and patted his shoulder from across the table. "Can you tell me anything about her that might help me find out who did this?"

Eric shook his head, not really declining, but just because he didn't know for sure. "We talked on the morning she disappeared. We were supposed to go to the movies that night, but I got into a big argument with Brooke. I ended up losing track of time while trying to calm things down at home. I accidentally stood Jessica up. When I finally remembered our date, I tried to call her, but she didn't answer the phone."

He wiped a couple of tears away with the palms of his hands and then blew his nose quietly into the napkin that had been wrapped around the silverware. "At first, I thought she was just mad at me, so I called a few more times. I left her a message on the answering machine, but she never called me back. I didn't think much of it, because it's not like we talked every day or anything. But then, a couple of days passed and I saw this poster hanging up at Medley's." He broke down again, and folded the poster back up, placing it into his jacket again with shaking hands.

Detective Darrow patted his shoulder some more and stared down at the floor beneath the table. He knew that the situation was really unusual, but he could feel Eric's sincerity. He'd seen so many guilty people before, and this wasn't one of them. Still, he needed to question things.

"Can you tell me about those scars on your hands?" he asked.

"Oh, these?" Eric sniffled and extended his hands onto the table, palms down. "That barber, Benji — I'm sure you know him — he was teaching me how to sharpen blades the right way. I inherited a bunch of antique knives when my grandpa passed, but they were dull and rusted. I heard that Benji was pretty good at that sort of stuff, so I asked him to help me learn how to restore them. I ended up not being very good at it, apparently."

Detective Darrow inhaled deeply. "Benji? Hmm."

Chapter 15

"Murder, She Wrote"

Saturday was much colder than Friday. Alice shivered as she stepped out of the shower and reached for her towel. The water that remained in her hair cooled instantly when the air touched it, causing her skin to cover itself with tiny goosebumps.

"I thought the weather was getting warmer, not colder," she thought to herself. *"I wonder if that's why this place is called Wintersburg. It's always so damn cold."*

She shivered from within her little makeshift cotton cocoon for a moment and then continued to dry herself off, making sure to soak up every last drop of icy water. The bathroom mirror was foggy from the steam, so she wiped away at its surface with the side of one of her hands. Her reflection became visible for a brief moment, before fogging over again.

Alice walked to her room and started rummaging around in her closet for something nice to wear. Tiffany had convinced her to go out again. She wanted to look a little more presentable than the last time, especially considering that Kirt's Pub would be even more packed than the previous night. It was always wild on the weekends.

She was eager for another night out, even though Detective Darrow had hinted that she should stay inside after she'd told him about her plans. He had expressed that he didn't think it was a good idea for any young woman to be out at night anymore, especially not at the bar. Alice didn't completely disagree with his opinion, but she didn't want to spend her life waiting around. She decided that she'd much rather live than to simply survive. Besides, she still intended on being careful while there, and after just a few drinks — and maybe a little bit of dancing — she'd be on her way back home. It seemed like a solid plan.

She quickly finished getting ready, and then walked next door to Tiffany's house.

Tiffany stepped out and locked the door. Her copper hair was teased a little more than usual, and she looked like she was ready to have a wild night. "Let's get out of here," she said in a singsongy voice. "Look. I put on my dancing shoes!"

Alice looked down and watched Tiffany tap her feet on the concrete porch, playfully. The shoes were definitely unique. They were bright red pumps with black checkered bows across the toe area. Needless to say, they were difficult to miss.

"Those are awesome!" Alice said, laughing. "I thought I was going to be the one sticking out with these hot pink heels, but it looks like you've got me beat."

Tiffany fluffed her hair in an exaggerated way and blew an imaginary kiss into the air. "As I always do, darling," she said, with a hysterically poor posh accent. "Besides, you wear those all the time. I'm sure people are used to seeing them by now."

"You're right, I guess."

Alice grinned and followed Tiffany to the car. She hopped into the passenger's side and used the mirror to touch up her lipstick one more time. It was good to see Tiffany so lively. It was so difficult to predict her moods sometimes.

The car chugged along for a few blocks until it reached the edge of town. The pub smelled strong as usual. The odor was so strong, in fact, it could be smelled from the gravel parking lot. The girls went inside and leaned against the bar top. All of the seats appeared to be taken for once, so they were left with no choice but to stay on their toes.

Kirt approached them, visibly stressed from the crowd. "What'll it be this time, ladies?" he asked, fanning himself with a stack of napkins as he spoke. Glistening lines of sweat decorated his tanned neck.

Even though the air was colder than usual outside, it was still hot and sticky inside the bar.

"Just a couple shots of whiskey, and a pitcher tonight," Tiffany replied.

"Alright then. Just a second." Kirt poured the drinks and then brought everything over to them. "It looks like that handsome barber is back," he said, motioning over to one of the pool tables. "I'd pay good money for him to do more than just run his hands through my hair if you know what I mean. He winked and continued staring at Benji.

A chill went down Alice's neck when she looked at him, and she shuddered. "He's pretty good looking, I guess, but he doesn't seem to have the best personality," she replied.

"Honey, with a body like that, does he really need anything else? As long as he's not completely insane, he's a keeper, as far as I'm concerned," he said, laughing, before walking away to refill some drinks for another group nearby.

Alice looked at Tiffany and noticed that she seemed a little less vivacious than she had been on the way over. "What's the matter? You seem tired all of a sudden."

"It's not that," she replied. "I just don't really like that guy very much. He dated Sarah for a while, but he always seemed like a total weirdo."

"What did he do that was so weird?" Alice asked, thinking back to her conversation with Roger. "Sarah's uncle told me that Benji didn't handle it very well when she broke things off with him. Is that true?"

Tiffany nodded. "That's really all it is, I guess. He never did anything too crazy, at least not that I heard about, but he always made me feel uncomfortable when he was around."

"Well, let's just forget about him. There are tons of people here. We can just ignore him and have a good night. It'll be like he's not even around. What do ya say?"

Tiffany smiled at the suggestion and straightened her posture. "You're right," she said. "Let's just forget about him and have some fun."

They raised their shot glasses into the air and gulped the liquid down. Tiffany hardly made a face, but Alice struggled to hide the fact that the whiskey had burned her throat.

"Kirt!" Tiffany yelled, "Two more, please!"

He gave her an enthusiastic thumbs-up and poured the girls another round.

***

After a couple of hours of laughter and dancing, the pair drove over to Medley's to pick up some snacks. While neither of them should have been behind the wheel after so much drinking, poor judgment had taken control of their actions. Fortunately, they made it to the store safely. They grabbed a few things to make sundaes, a few bags of chips, and some sodas, and then hurried to the cash register. Wonderbread Will was standing near the exit, pacing back and forth.

"That's Will," Tiffany whispered, trying not to make it obvious that she was talking about him. "I'll tell you more about him when we get back to my place."

Alice nodded and paid for the groceries. They hopped into the car and drove carefully to Tiffany's house. Once inside, Alice followed her into the kitchen and they sat the food down on the counter-top.

"Let's both just stay here tonight," Tiffany suggested. "We can eat all of this junk-food and see if there are any good movies on TV."

Alice was happy with the suggestion. "Sounds good to me," she replied. "Oh, and what did you want to tell me about that Will guy? I've seen him with Betty before, but I don't know much more about him."

"I almost forgot!" Tiffany exclaimed. "He was Sarah's uncle. Her mom, Betty, has been taking care of him for a while. He's a strange one."

"Roger spoke to me a little bit about that, but he didn't say much. What's wrong with him?" she asked.

"Well, I heard that he used to be pretty

normal when he was still a kid. Apparently he was playing baseball one day with Roger and his friends when he was about ten years old. The other boys were a couple of years older than him, so they were a little stronger. Roger was upset for some reason and threw the baseball bat, not realizing that Will was still standing right next to him. It flew in the air and cracked him right on the head! He had to stay in the hospital for a long time. Apparently, he has been a little strange ever since then."

"What? That can't be true" Alice replied. "Who told you that story? Someone's probably just pulling your leg... Can someone's personality even be changed from something like that?"

"Actually, Sarah told me all about it one night. I'm pretty sure it's true. She went on to explain that Roger has always felt responsible for his brother's issues, so that's why he pays for all of his bills and stuff. He seems to be tough on Will sometimes, but if you look a little deeper, you can see that he probably cares about him more than anyone else does."

"That's so awful," Alice said, shaking her head in disbelief. "I can't even imagine having the bear such guilt..."

Tiffany lit a cigarette and blew a small puff of smoke into the air. "Oh, it gets even sadder, believe me," she continued. "People have made up crazy stories about him over the years. Even though he's a grown man, the local kids still tease him all the time. I feel so bad for him whenever I see him walking around, always pulling that silly red wagon. He throws cans, and other things in it to sell at the recycling center for spare cash. I figured I'd point him out to you to let you know that he's actually pretty sweet, even if he seems scary sometimes. You know, since you've been a little anxious lately, too. I don't want you to get nervous if he says something weird to you. That's just how he is."

"Thanks for letting me know," she replied. "I really just wish people weren't so cruel to each other."

"Me too," Tiffany said while flicking ash into a little glass tray. "People are pretty evil sometimes." She finished her cigarette and changed the subject. "Anyway, let's not dwell on sad stuff anymore tonight. Let's make these sundaes," she abruptly suggested. "But first, let's do one more shot. I have some more whiskey on the shelf above the sink."

Tiffany walked over and giggled as she poured a small amount into two empty coffee cups. She handed one to Alice. They both threw their heads back in unison and gulped it all down quickly. After, Alice put her cup on the counter and reached into the grocery bags. She pulled out all of the items they'd bought and examined the assortment.

"Crap. How could we have forgotten the whipped cream and cherries?"

"What? No way..." Tiffany said, surprised. "We definitely can't risk driving now, either."

"You wait here and find us a movie to watch, okay?" Alice suggested. "I'll walk back over to Medley's really quick to get what we need."

"Hmm, I'm not sure about that. You know it's not safe out there, Alice."

"It's whatever. I'll be fine. Just give me your flashlight and I'll be back before you can even miss me."

Tiffany nodded and tossed her the flashlight from the drawer.

With both of their judgment impaired, it really didn't seem like such a bad idea for Alice to be alone in the night's darkness. They were both sober enough to be concerned, but too inebriated to take more caution.

"You've got thirty minutes, kid, and then I'm going out to find you."

"Deal!" Alice said. "I probably won't even be gone for twenty of those minutes anyway." She shoved the flashlight into her purse and walked out the door.

***

Alice made it all the way to the store without any issues, aside from a little bit of stumbling along the way. After she paid, she started her journey back to the house with a can of whipped cream, and a jar full of sweet sticky red cherries stuffed into a grocery bag. She swung them around daintily as she turned the corner, leaving Medley's parking lot.

A car drove up beside her, illuminating the entire street with its bright yellow lights. It continued to drive for several more feet before it came to a stop just a little bit ahead of her. She could see the silhouette of a person leaning over to the passenger's side, cranking the window down.

She considered crossing to the other side of the street, but her legs continued to carry her in the direction of the car. Just as she was becoming a little nervous, a voice called out to her from inside of it.

"What are you doing walking around out here all alone at this hour?" the man's voice asked, trying to sound friendly. He wasn't able to mask his concern entirely.

"Blake! You made me nervous. Um, I forgot to pick up a few things and had to run out really fast. It's not a huge deal." She walked up to the window to see him face-to-face. She was used to seeing him inside of his patrol car — not in his personal one.

He smiled and pointed to the door. "Hop in. I'll take you home." He paused to look at the grocery bag, and then raised an eyebrow. "What was so important that you needed to walk to the store alone, and —" He inhaled sharply before continuing his sentence. "— while smelling like you took a bath in bourbon?"

Alice laughed for a moment and pushed her fluffy hair out of her face. It had tangled a lot over the course of the night, and the damp evening air had made her hair products turn into a sticky film that coated each teased strand like fragrant honey.

"Well, this is going to sound kind of stupid, I guess, but I needed some toppings for sundaes."

Detective Darrow's face went blank, and his voice sounded flat. "You're out here... for sundaes?" A little bit of life's confusion found itself in his tone, and he was suddenly full of questions. "For sundaes... Are you kidding me right now? Who thinks that ice-cream is an emergency? I mean, I'm not your boss. You can do whatever you want, but...

really?"

He let out a small laugh and peeked into the bag.

"Whipped cream," he said, raising his eyebrow with a little more interest than the last time. "Are you sure you got this for sundaes?"

She smacked him playfully on the shoulder. "What else would it be for?" she asked, knowing exactly what was going through his mind.

He shrugged and smiled.

"And what's with that smirk? Don't make me cover it up!" She reached into the bag and pulled out the can, taking the lid off quickly. She pointed the nozzle toward Detective Darrow like a weapon that she was fully intending on using.

"You wouldn't dare," he dared.

"Then you don't know me as well as you think you do." She swung the can toward his mouth and squirted a glob of whipped cream across his lips and chin. Most of it fell onto his shirt and into his lap, making a mess. She fell back into the seat, and belly-laughed, wiping tears away from her eyes with the knuckles on her free hand. "I'm so sorry," she said between breathy laughs. "I didn't think that much would come out all at once."

Detective Darrow unbuckled his seatbelt and reached over the center console. He wrestled the metal can out of Alice's hands and sprayed her with it in return.

Whipped cream went all over her hair, face, and clothes, and she immediately started wiping away at the mess.

"What the hell, Blake? Oh, you're in trouble now!" she yelped excitedly.

He slid back into his seat and held the can out of her reach. She leaned over and tried to grab it from him. Detective Darrow stared up at her smiling face, and admired how beautiful she looked, even though she was completely disheveled and sticky. He let her succeed in grabbing the whipped cream. As soon as it was in her hands, his fingers cupped her tangled mane, and he pulled her face into his. Their lips met for several minutes.

Alice sat back into her seat, breathing heavily. "I really need to get back. Tiffany's really going to be worried if I'm gone much longer. I told her I'd only be a few minutes."

"Yeah, sure. Uh —"

"Uh what?" she asked, curious.

"How are you going to explain this?" He held up the empty can.

She smiled and shook her head. "I guess I'll just say that I dropped it. Apparently it wasn't so important after all."

"Told you so," he said, still wearing that shit-eating grin.

He pulled back onto the street and drove in the direction of Tiffany's house. Sweat and humidity had produced a thin layer of steam across all of the windows and windshield, but he was able to see through a small bare patch in front of the steering wheel. It slowly cleared as he reached the house.

"Thanks for dropping me off, and —" Alice paused to think of the words. "— and for spending some time with me. We'll have to meet up again soon."

Detective Darrow cut the engine. "Let me walk you to the door, at least."

"Oh wow, such a gentleman," she said with a mixture of sarcasm and amusement. "I think I'd actually like that."

They stepped up onto Tiffany's porch, and he leaned in for a quick kiss.

"Sorry, I just had to steal one more before saying goodbye," he said while peering his head over to the window next to the door. The blinds had been opened completely. "I don't know how your friend would react if she knew you were late because of me, so I'd better get out of h —" he froze, and his eyes widened.

Alice turned to see what had startled him.

Through the window, a large puddle of blood was visible. It coated the floor like glossy red wax. Red handprints and other smudges were all over the walls.

Detective Darrow barged through the door and ran inside. Even without his gun, he was fearless and ready to fight.

Alice stayed close behind him, keeping watch from behind as they followed a long trail of blood to the bedroom. It looked as if someone had been dragged all the way there. Drops and tiny crimson beads littered the path, along with more smudges and handprints. It became apparent that the person hadn't actually been dragged at all. They'd pulled themselves into the room.

At the end of the trail, Tiffany rested. Her body was face-down, but her flame-colored hair identified her on its own. She still wore the same outfit as before, but her shirt was pulled up and wrapped tightly around her neck.

Detective Darrow rolled her over, and she gurgled. He loosened the shirt, allowing her airway to have some room to breathe, but it was already too late. She looked over at

Alice with fear in her eyes, but her pupils became less and less wild until all of the fire had drained out of her.

Alice fell to the floor and sobbed. She held Tiffany's hand and pleaded to her lifeless body.

***

During the following night, nightmares disturbed what little sleep Alice had been able to get. She had tossed and turned in between unpleasant visions and exaggerated details of Tiffany's murder. Her mind had made up its own ideas of what had really happened, and it played them back to her like a film that she'd never agreed upon seeing.

Once the dreams of Tiffany had passed, Alice was greeted with one final story-line. She fell into a deeper sleep and saw Sarah. A deep tangible sadness was upon her face, and the air around her smelled damp and mossy. Alice shivered from under the covers, with both of her eyes still closed.

Sarah's hand guided her to the basement door, and down the stairs.

Alice stared at her for directions, but Sarah was growing more and more upset until tears started to stream down both of her cheeks. She was silent, but her pain could still be heard regardless. She froze at the bottom of the steps and pointed to the cardboard box in the corner of the room.

Alice walked over to it, glancing back one time to make sure that she was following the instructions properly. She squatted to the floor and opened the box. Sarah walked up to her side and waited while she sifted through the photographs on top.

Suddenly, Sarah's hand raised again, and she pointed to a family photo.

"What are you trying to tell me?" Alice asked. She looked at the picture again and saw Sarah, Betty, Roger, and Will staring up at her with happy faces. She didn't remember seeing this photo when she'd gone through the stack before. Her fingers ran across the names that had been handwritten on the back, and then she turned to Sarah again.

No one was there.

Chapter 16

"Every Breath You Take"

It was one of those hot summer mornings where the sun beamed down upon the earth as if it had been looking to set the entire thing ablaze. Clouds were nowhere in sight, and the bright natural light illuminated every piece of exposed land, leaving very few places behind that were able to keep any shadowy secrets intact. Alice pulled into the salon's parking lot and cut her engine. She wore her hair up and out of her face, with little effort put into the styling. Sunglasses rested across the top of her head, helping to pull her bangs out of her swollen eyes. Her hands hovered over the steering wheel as she tried to decide on whether or not to stay in the car and drive back home or to go inside and face the world with responsibility.

She wasn't even entirely sure of which option was the most admirable, or why that even mattered. She wasn't sure if anything mattered at all anymore, in fact. Life felt so fragile all of a sudden, and almost even pointless. While she had no desire to die, herself, everything she'd once enjoyed had been tainted with gloom.

She lit a cigarette and held it loosely between her poorly painted lips. Smoking wasn't typically a vice of her own, but she'd grabbed the pack from Tiffany's kitchen counter when she was helping to clean up the mess that had been left behind. She hadn't felt as if she were allowed to take anything of value, so all she had taken was the single box of smokey sentiment. Alice brought a lighter up to the tip and lit it quickly. She took a few long puffs and leaned back a little in her seat.

"I can do this," she thought. *"I can't just keep sitting around."*

She lifted a foot into her seat and brought the knee toward her chest. Her arm perched itself on top of her leg like a clumsy bird, and she continued smoking. All of the courage that she had mustered while getting ready had started to dissipate. She batted at the keys that were dangling from the ignition, and she considered the options over and over again. Her eyes scanned the dashboard, but they hadn't really been searching for anything specific. They stopped moving the moment that they reached Sarah's yellow bow. Alice had thrown it up there a while back and had completely forgotten about it.

"Maybe this will make me look a little more put together," she thought as she removed the sunglasses from her hair, replacing them with the new accessory.

She checked the time on her thin golden watch and realized that she was already a few minutes late. The cars in the parking lot should have been enough indication of that, but she hadn't really noticed them when she was pulling in. She slid her leg back down to the floor and smashed the butt of her cigarette into the car's barely-used ashtray. Her thoughts wandered off to the kiss that she'd shared with Detective Darrow, and she felt a little more at ease. Even though it had been very unexpected, she'd felt genuinely happy in that moment with him. How sad it was that such a moment had to be ruined by an almost indescribable tragedy. With everything that had been going on since she and Detective Darrow discovered Tiffany murdered in her own home, she hadn't even taken the time to dissect the entire romantic encounter that they had shared together. To be completely honest, she hadn't even really thought back on it at all until that very moment in her car. She wondered if the kiss had crossed his mind, or if it had slipped away and been buried underneath the stress of the accumulating bodies.

Alice reached into her purse and pulled out her lipstick. In a desperate attempt to look a little less shaken and worn, she rubbed the smudged color from her lips onto her wrist and reapplied it with more precision. She felt some mixed feelings for beautifying herself while she was still mourning. It felt shameful to be vain when her friend's lips had turned pale and blue at the hands of death's makeup artist, but she didn't want people to think she looked haggard.

A single fluffy cloud formed out of nowhere in the sky above, partially blanketing the sun. It was pale and milky, and it cooled the blazing yellow star like a big scoop of vanilla ice-cream. Alice stared out from the windows of her car and looked all around at the various buildings nearby. There were tiny shops with markings all across the buildings where the bricks had once displayed the different lettering of the many businesses before.

Nothing lasted in Wintersburg — not even the people, apparently. For a town that was so known for being trapped in time, for being something like a capsule that was hidden far away from malls, hotels, and fancy restaurants, many of its things seemed so fleeting.

Alice sighed and pulled her key out the ignition. It chimed as it smashed into the others on her keychain, and she shoved them all deep into her purse. Her arm reached out to her side, and she opened the car door, turning her body slowly just in case her mind was to change. Her thoughts wandered to the group of girls who stood together like a flock of geese, waiting for their school bus. They giggled together and helped each other with their hair, swapping their accessories out for new ones. The sight of them took her back to her younger years, where she had often found herself wishing for friends like that. She wasn't ever entirely alone, but she'd lacked the closeness that many girls her age had found among one another. Those sleepover nights, where friends would eat junk food without any fear of weight gain, gossiping about which boy was the cutest, and prank calling all of the neighbors and teachers — these were the things she regretted missing out on, and these were the things she had just started to find in Tiffany.

The loss of Tiffany had cut Alice almost as deeply as her grandmother's had. It only cut her in a different place. Losing her grandmother felt a lot like losing her childhood. Losing Tiffany felt more like getting that childhood back and then waking to realize that it had all just been a dream.

And now, she was alone again.

Her mind stopped wandering, and she stood up, closing the car's door behind her. Her feet carried her to the entrance of the salon, and she opened the heavy door. The bell sang to her like a voice out of tune, before it stopped as quickly as it had started. She straightened her posture and tried to look up with a dignified chin. If she could fake the confidence for long enough, she would be able to push through how intensely uncomfortable everything was, at least, in theory. Everything had been going smoothly until she reached her station. It was almost as if the moment that her combs hit the counter, the gossip started.

"I just can't believe it," a voice whispered in a harsh tone. "How many girls have to die before someone responsible in this town does something about it? I swear these cops are completely incompetent."

"I know. There's no excuse anymore. They should at least have a suspect by now. There's barely a thousand people in this place, and we're losing more and more of them while those boys sit in their office, eating pizza and watching TV. It's all on our dime, too!"

Alice tried to ignore the whispering, but the voices grew louder and more confident as she stood there, quietly and quickly setting up her supplies for the day.

"That redhead didn't even look like the others, so they can't blame it on someone having a type anymore," a third voice chimed in. "They need to go back and take more prints if you ask me."

Alice thought it was kind of amusing that the strongest opinions tended to come from the people who knew the least about the subject at hand. It was as if they were trying to fill in the blanks by speaking louder and producing as many words as possible to stuff into the large void between their ears.

The more words that they said, the more information the people felt like they knew. And the angrier that they seemed, the more likely it was that the others would listen to what they had to say. Even Alice knew that having a hive-mind was a dangerous and damaging thing, especially when the hive didn't know what it was working toward, or even what it was fighting against.

She tried not to let the women phase her with their ridicule. Sure, she agreed that the cops could have been doing a little more to solve the case, but their resources were limited, and the county sheriff and his deputies had only just started their investigation. A group of people could only do so much in such a short amount of time, and they could do even less when forensics and murder were involved. Finding a serial killer wasn't a task as simple as writing someone a speeding ticket.

"The cops are doing all that they can, I'm sure," Edna's voice broke through the crowd. Her silver hair shined like freshly polished silver. Her personality sparkled just as brightly among the room full of dowdy jean muumuu dresses, and overly powdered faces. She wore high-waisted pleated slacks, and a daring sharp shouldered blouse, making her look like she could have been Madonna's fairy godmother. Only, instead of a magic wand, she waved a half-lit cigarette in the air as she walked onto the main floor, entering the room like it was her stage. Her plum-colored lipstick stained the orange filter more and more each time she inhaled its smoke as if she had been using it as a makeup blotting tool. Her short pointed toed shoes clomped on the floor with authority, and she swayed her hips to match their confident sound.

"Are you doing alright, Alice?" she asked, with her free hand placed onto her thin hip.

Alice nodded and replied, "Yeah, I think so."

"Good. Now, you let me know if anyone's yapping starts to bother you. I'm not in the mood to be messed with today, and I won't be putting up with anyone messing with you either. It takes real discipline to show up to work after witnessing such a thing. Don't let anyone suggest anything otherwise."

Edna spoke with sass and attitude, making sure her voice was heard across the salon. She spoke as if she had heard the women speaking behind Alice's back. And she had, actually. She heard them talking right before Alice had walked in for her shift. The clients had already been spouting out their theories. One of them had even gone as far as to mention how strange of a coincidence it was for Alice to have been gone for the perfect amount of time during Tiffany's brutal attack. "How convenient," the horrid old woman had said with suspicion in her tone.

Edna was beyond just sitting back and

letting the women enjoy their makeshift therapy sessions anymore. Gossip was fairly harmless on its own, but rumors could quickly turn into suggestions, and suggestions were capable of turning into something as equal as facts in the eyes of squawking bitter women. With nothing else to occupy their time, judgment had become their hobby, but Edna wasn't going to allow Alice to stand trial that day. The sins that the women spoke of were someone else's, and she wasn't going to entertain the thought of standing by to allow a crucifixion to take place in her salon — at least not Alice's, anyway.

"Thank you," Alice said quietly, but with great appreciation. "I'm just trying to push through it all and keep going like nothing happened right now."

"And that's all you need to do," Edna replied, nodding approvingly.

***

Alice made it through the rest of her shift without hearing hardly a peep from anyone else. The few words that she had been able to hear were still lingering around in her mind though, as she drove back in the direction of her house.

Tiffany's mailbox soon came into view, and Alice tried not to stare or think about the letters that her friend would never be able to read, and the stacks of solicitations that were already beginning to pile up. The mailman must have not been told to stop delivering to her address, because the letters still arrived each day, waiting for Tiffany's parents to find them. It annoyed Alice that even in death, a person was unable to escape an ever-growing hoard of junk mail. Why anyone would want to sell snake oil to a dead person was beyond her imagination.

She finally emerged from her hot car, glistening with sweat and smelling salty like summertime. The sun was about to go down, but she didn't want her mood to sink along with it. To combat her emotions, she hummed the chorus of a popular love song as she stepped onto the porch. She paused to sigh heavily as she went through each of her keys to find the one for the front door and then resumed the pleasant humming. This task should have been easy by now, but nothing really was so simple anymore. She managed to unlock the door and stepped inside her home, and then into her living room.

The air smelled different. Her nose picked up on the change when she had turned to close the door. Her hand felt around on the wall for the light switch, and in a single click, the room was suddenly brightened.

Alice looked around, slowly adjusting to the change from natural to artificial light, and she saw someone sitting on the couch right next to her. A chill went down her neck and back, making the small specks of sweat that clung to her peach fuzz freeze like small rounded icicles. Her heart felt as if someone had stunned it, or as if an imaginary switch had been flipped to stop it from beating. The switch must have been turned back on just as quickly though because her heart started to race with more force than it ever had before. Her knees grew weak and shaky from all of the adrenaline, and they were practically begging for her to start running. The rest of her body had made the decision to focus on fighting instead of fleeing though.

"Benji," she thought. The name itself might as well have been a complete story of its own. She mustered up the courage to speak.

"W — what are you doing in my house?" she asked with a shaking and stammering voice.

Benji put his hands on his knees and leaned forward, bringing himself up to his feet. He took a single step toward her and grinned largely. His hair was an absolute mess as if he had been sitting in front of an industrial fan, and his face was covered in stubble. The bags under his eyes made him appear as if he hadn't slept for days. His sour decay-laced breath confirmed that he probably hadn't washed himself for a while either.

"I've been waiting for you," he said, with his voice raspier than usual. He cleared his throat and softened his tone. "I waited here all day, actually."

Alice's eyes went wild as she watched him take another step forward. The only thing separating her from him was a space that was only about the size of a grave. She tried to be brave. "How'd you get in here, Benji? What do you want?"

His eyes lit up with amusement, and his eyebrows raised so much that he looked like a caricature of himself. Nothing about him seemed to be real at that moment, but he was still there in the flesh. His arms raised out toward her, and he flapped his fingers into his palms as if he were telling Alice to approach him.

"Oh, steady now..." he began, tauntingly. "We've got ourselves a tough girl today, huh? I saw that you fixed the lock on the back door, so I checked all of the windows. You forgot to lock the one in your bedroom. You really didn't think that I'd notice if you stayed out all day? Who do you think I am, Sarah? I care about you more than anyone else does."

"Sarah?" Alice thought, very confused.

"Come here, baby," he continued, taking a couple more steps toward her until he was only inches away from her. "I was so upset when I saw you sucking face with that cop. I almost couldn't stop myself from interfering."

"You were spying on me? What the hell is wrong with you?"

"I saw you leave the bar with that redhead and wanted to see where you two were going. I didn't expect you to take a walk to the grocery so late. What was the whipped cream for?"

"That's none of your —"

"You don't need to tell me," he interrupted. "I got to see it all for myself. You're lucky I was too hurt to bust the windows out. Imagine how it felt to see my girl licking slop from some pig's face? It was like someone kicked me right in the gut. I mean, I could barely breathe. I have to admit something though. After I calmed down, it turned me on a little."

Benji breathed his foul breath into her face.

When Alice stumbled backward, he

caught her by the loose fabric at her waist, and yanked her back toward him, pulling her in close to his own body. She lifted a hand to push away at his chest, but he cupped her face with his palms. Her skull was squeezed tightly between his dry mitts, and no matter how hard she clawed away at his fingers, his grip never loosened from her cheekbones or jaw. The tips of his pinkies dug themselves deeper and deeper into the pressure points behind her ears.

"Why have you been ignoring me, Sarah?" he asked. "I've been calling you every day. I've been stopping by so much too. Where have you been? Why don't you kiss me like that anymore?"

"I'm not Sarah!" Alice yelled with terror. "I'm Alice, you fucking idiot!" She clawed at his hands and fingers even more, desperately trying to pull them away from her head.

Tears of fright escaped from her eyes, and they dripped down her cheeks and onto Benji's wrists. Their warmth seemed to satisfy some of his aggressive urges.

"Baby," his voice cooed out with a sudden softness as if he were trying to comfort an injured pet. "Don't say these things. You know it hurts my feelings when you call me names."

Alice stopped fighting his grip and

realized that more drastic measures were necessary. Clearly, Benji was completely out of his mind, and she had no idea what he could be capable of doing in such a state. He was obsessed with a ghost, and Alice was just her apparition. To him, Alice was his orb to hold and coddle.

She lifted her leg, and the heel of her favorite pink high heel slammed down onto the tongue of his gym shoe and buried itself into the top of his foot. He immediately let go of her and reached down to grab the wound.

Alice turned to run toward the door, taking the opportunity to escape the situation, but Benji lunged forward, with his long arms catching her by the back of her blouse this time. Using his other hand, he grabbed her brunette ponytail and yanked her head down toward her shoulder blades.

Immediately, she felt a sharp pain in the back of her neck.

Benji pulled her over toward him again and brought her down to the ground. He climbed on top of her, pinning her beneath his lap. Using his weight, he held her arms underneath him to keep her from fighting back again.

"You really shouldn't have done that, baby girl," he taunted, his voice sickly sweet. "Now I'm going to have to punish you." He covered her mouth with one hand, and wrapped the other loosely across her throat, hovering above her most important veins.

His eyes were large and stared at her like two black holes that were trying to suck every atom of her body into their depths. "Did it mean nothing to you? I know we really had something, and I'm not just going to sit back and let it become some pathetic memory. You can't make a man feel things like that, and then just throw him away like he's just a toy you no longer want. I'm not that easy to replace. I won't be."

Alice wiggled her head, trying to scream, but all of her sounds were muffled. "I'm not Sarah! I'm not Sarah! I'm Alice!" she tried to yell, over and over.

"I'm going to give you some options," he said while leaning in closely. Sweat dripped from his forehead and landed inside of Alice's eyes. "You can either apologize and be with me again, and we can forget all about this little scuffle, or you can keep resisting and I'll have to break you like a horse. What'll it be, Sarah? Will you give me another chance, or are you going to make me change your mind myself? I'm not afraid to be convincing if I have to be."

He tightened his grip and Alice immediately felt herself losing oxygen. But as soon as her vision darkened, Benji let go and uncovered her mouth for an answer.

"I'm not Alice! My name is —" she said quickly.

He quickly brought his hand back down into her face, bloodying her nose from the impact. She squirmed and cried through the spaces between his fingers.

He grasped her throat once more, and made an exaggeratedly sad expression, mocking her pain. "It really is a shame. I just can't bear the thought of having anyone else touch you though. I'm so sorry it had to be this way." he said, tightening his hand again. "Sleep well, Sarah. Wait for me by the gates. I'll only be a few minutes behind you."

***

Detective Darrow drove past Alice's house in his cruiser. A hot pizza sat in his passenger's seat, along with a 2-liter of soda. Even though he was still on duty, he figured that no one would notice if he took a few minutes out of his day to comfort Alice. After all, she'd gone through a lot, and it seemed like a responsible thing to go and check on her. He saw her car in the driveway, and he parked on the side of the street, leaving his keys in the ignition and the engine still running.

"I'll just be a second," he reminded

himself as he approached the front door, holding the food. He lifted his fist to knock but paused when he heard loud thudding sounds inside, as well as a male's voice. He put his ear to the door and listened more closely.

"It won't hurt for long. I promise," the male voice said, followed by Alice's muffled shrieks. "Just stop fighting it."

Detective Darrow dropped the pizza box and turned the doorknob. It was unlocked. He leaped inside and didn't even pause to analyze the situation before reacting. Instinct took over his entire body, and he wrestled Benji away from Alice like a hyena fighting for scraps. Benji fought back and reached into his pocket as soon as Detective Darrow had him held down to the floor.

He lifted a straight razor — the one that he had used to shave many necks before, and swiped it across Detective Darrow's bicep, cutting him deeply. Blood immediately poured out all over both of them, but the fight still continued.

Alice scooted herself backward toward the kitchen, holding her swollen throat in shock. She managed to reach for the phone and lifted herself up to dial 9-1-1. With what little voice she could muster up, she said her address, and then let go. The phone dangled from the cord, bobbing around like a giant fishing lure.

She fell back down to the floor.

Chapter 17

"No Way Out"

Tuesday, November 15ᵗʰ, 1988

The summer felt like a distant memory, and autumn would soon feel like the same. Alice sat in front of her TV, dressed and ready for work. The women at the salon had finally stopped talking about Benji getting arrested, and how the town was safe again. They'd moved onto other annoying topics.

Alice flipped absentmindedly through the channels, waiting a while until it was time to face the day again. She'd been forcing herself to get ready early so she could have enough time to collect her thoughts before each shift. Socializing was more difficult than it had ever been, but she wore her mask of confidence just as well as she had worn it before. No one knew that the person who hid behind it was still injured and afraid. Deep down inside, she was still the eleven-year-old version of herself who had feared scrutiny.

She recalled the summer that she had been invited to her friend's twelfth birthday party. Her friend, Laura, lived outside of the city, in a house that was surrounded by woods and farmland. The girl's parents had grown crops and were well-off enough to not have to worry about the expense of driving Laura back and forth to her 7th-grade classes each day. Even so, they still weren't interested in sending her off to study in a private school. They had wanted Laura to grow up exposed to other kids who didn't have as much. They wanted her to see the brown-bagged lunches and the hand-me-down clothes, so she could be more aware and appreciative of the things she had at home. The exposure didn't exactly work, and it just made Laura act as if she were better than everyone else instead.

Alice had shown up to the girl's party with her hair still damp, and with a small doll wrapped in modest wrapping paper held tightly in her hands. There were no bows or frills attached to the gift, but it was still fairly presentable. When Laura had opened it, she laughed in front of everyone, putting Alice down for thinking that a girl her age would still play with dolls. The other girls joined in on the laughter, and Alice eventually walked off toward the group of boys who had been tossing balls back and forth in the yard. She needed a break from the taunting.

She had recognized one of the guys from her lunch table. His name was George, and he was a strange creature. He always knew the latest foul phrases and bad words, and could often be found smoking in the locker room at school. Despite his bad-boy image, he'd always been nice to Alice.

When he had suggested that they should go into the woods to explore alone, she hadn't thought much of it. She followed him for several minutes until they'd lost sight of the path that they'd initially taken. Alice had gotten nervous and suggested that they should turn around, so no one would worry, and the boy agreed with her. But, instead of leading her the correct way, he led her deeper and deeper into the woods, even farther away from civilization. The twigs and thorns scraped against Alice's legs as she obeyed his navigation, and he eventually left her there after saying that he would be right back. They had already been gone for a couple of hours, and the sky had darkened during that time. She had felt more and more afraid as the sun disappeared into the darkness.

Finally, in the distance, she heard her name being called, and she cried out for help.

George stood in the back of the group with the rest of the boys, beaming, and they all giggled at the sight of her. The girls started to scold her for being a slut, and she didn't understand what was going on or what they were talking about at first. She followed the group back to the house, something that took nearly thirty minutes, and then she walked inside.

Laura's dad poured a cold glass of water for George and patted him on the back, approving of something. No one gave Alice anything to drink though, despite her mentioning that she was very thirsty. They only told her to go and wait outside while they called her grandmother to come and pick her up. As time went on, she heard the rumors about herself in the school hallways, and both the girls and the guys avoided her for the remainder of the year.

Alice shook the intrusive thoughts

from her head and turned the TV off. She needed to focus on happier things.

***

It was around the time that Alice's shift at the salon had ended that she felt a wave of dread pour over her. The doctors had told her that these feelings would be common while she was still emotionally healing from the encounter with Benji, but this feeling was different than the others. It felt more immediate. Whatever it was, she pushed it off to the side anyway and drove over to Betty's house. She had promised her that she would do her hair that day, and she didn't want to let her down. Alice's car turned into Betty's winding gravel driveway, and she followed it all the way behind the house, in view of the lake. The breeze felt nice across her face as she exited her vehicle. She stood there, quietly, and let it pass across her cheeks like cold silk before she walked up to the back door.

She knocked a few times, but there was no answer. Betty's car was in the driveway, so she knew that she was home.

"Oh boy, I hope she's not drunk this time," Alice thought to herself.

She made the decision to walk down to

the lake. Due to all of the negativity surrounding the once-loved body of water, she had avoided it much like the other people in town. She passed a large shed as she made her way to the mud and rocks, wondering what sort of weird things might be inside of it. If the shed was anything like Betty's living room, it was probably full of bags of garbage, and empty wine bottles. The scent in the air confirmed that she could have been correct, but it was most likely just the stench of dead animals. After all, Betty and Will had to butcher their pigs somewhere. It only made sense that they had a shed for such things.

She racked her brain, trying to think of what Betty could have possibly been doing at that moment. They'd talked on the phone during Alice's lunch break and had confirmed that she was going to stop by afterward, just as usual.

A small flat stone caught her eye, and she decided to toss a few into the water to see if she could get any of them to skip across. She hadn't tried doing that since she was just a child, but she felt confident in her ability to succeed. After a few flops and failures, she was able to get one to hop across the water like a frog skipping lily pads. Alice closed her eyes and felt the cloud-darkened sun on her cheeks. Even though winter was close by again, there was just enough warmth and hope remaining in the lake and air. She felt completely relaxed for the first time in quite a while.

She opened her eyes once more and reached down for another stone. The one that she grabbed was much less flat than the others that surrounded her. Its edges were rounded, and it seemed to hook around her entire hand like a light-weight horseshoe. She looked down to see what she was holding onto.

In her hand, she held onto a partially broken jawbone. It was unmistakably human and had a few molars still intact. Alice stumbled backward but caught her balance before she could fall. She dropped the bone to the ground, and it made a light tapping sound as it hit the rocks.

"Oh my God," she whispered.

Footsteps approached her from behind. Before she could react, she heard a loud crack. A large rock, about the size of a barn cat, fell down next to her and landed on top of the bone. A tooth was knocked loose from the impact and it flew up toward her ankle before falling back down again next to the rock. Alice collapsed to the ground as well, landing beside it. Terrified, she rolled over with her hands raised in front of her face and screamed as loud as she could.

Will stood above her, giggling in a mocking sort of way, and pulled a large pair of garden shears from his back pocket. He had come prepared. He squatted down beside her and grabbed a handful of her dark hair in his dirt-covered paws.

"Don't move," he said flatly, as he sawed through the hair with the dull blades, mumbling about his mother. "Mama will love this," he repeated to himself. "Mama will be so proud of me this time."

Alice screamed and ripped into his arms with her long fake nails. One popped off from the impact, and another broke into pieces, creating a sharp edge. They sank into his skin like shark teeth, leaving long trailing marks all the way down to his wrists. Will dropped the shears and Alice's hair fell into a loose pile, dispersing like sand upon impact.

He grabbed the large rock once more and brought it down onto Alice's head without hesitation. "You're too loud," he said.

Alice's vision flashed on and off as if someone were resetting the breaker in her brain over and over again. She thought of her basement, and how often she had to go down there to do just that. Sarah's belongings crossed her mind next, and her silhouette suddenly appeared before Alice, running toward her through each of the flashes of light.

In what seemed like only a few seconds, she saw that Sarah's eyes were staring into hers. They looked absolutely terrified. Alice watched as her lips started moving, but was surprised to hear Betty's voice come out from them. As she continued staring, she saw Sarah's face age a few decades, until it ultimately became Betty's as well.

"We can't keep doing this! We just can't do this anymore, Will! Put it down! Put the damn rock down!" Betty yelped, sobbing as she fell to her knees.

Will dropped the rock a final time, and the lights finally stopped flashing for Alice.

***

Several hours must have passed by because Alice opened her eyes to see very little in the night's darkness. There were cracks in between the pieces of wood. They let in just enough moonlight through to allow her to be able to see that she was inside of a shed. It took a few more moments for Alice to realize that this was actually the large shed that she had passed by earlier on her way down to the water. The odor was even more putrid from the inside. What had only smelled foul when she was out in the backyard, now smelled like blood and decay. She closed her eyes once again, hoping that she was just dreaming.

She stayed in somewhat of a daze, fading in and out of consciousness for the rest of the evening. All semblance of time had been lost to her in the darkness and cold. When thin rays of sunlight slipped through the shed's water-logged lumber, Alice was able to see her surroundings more clearly. She looked down at her sore wrists. They were tied to her ankles, forcing her to either fall sideways into the fetal position or to sit with her torso slightly slouched over her knees. Her joints ached in protest.

"It's already morning," she thought, with stressful reality pouring over her like a cold shower. *"I need to find a way out of here."* Fear filled Alice's mind, and adrenaline kicked back into her bloodstream.

She began searching the room for anything that she could use to cut the rope that had been keeping her restrained. She wobbled across the shed, inching her way over to a long table that was pushed all the way against the wall in the back. When she reached it, she realized that it held nothing other than chopped up pig guts and little bits of bone. Despite the evidence of a knife's existence, there wasn't a single one in sight. She looked underneath the table to be completely sure, but she saw something unexpected instead. Several dehydrated human toes were pushed back against the wall as if they had been overlooked when cleaning at some point. They appeared to have been swept away quickly and forgotten about. Their toenails were black, but not polished. They were colored only by death's natural and more odorous lacquer.

Alice panicked. She tried to scoot back as quickly as she could, but she fell to her side instead. With panting breaths, she brought her knees to her chest and wailed loudly. In her entire life, she had never felt so afraid — not even on the night when Benji had put his hands around her throat. Just as a long and deep whinny came out of her mouth, the shed door started to shake and rattle. Betty appeared in the distance, with her shadowy silhouette looking menacing in front of the sun.

"Oh, you're awake now?" she asked, seeming surprised as she approached Alice. "That's good." She held onto a paper plate with some sort of noodle-filled slop on it. Squatting to her knees, she pulled a fork out of her back pocket and scooped some of the mess in front of Alice's mouth. "Sit up and eat this, or I'll shovel it down your throat myself," she said. She didn't seem like she was joking either.

When Alice leaned her head down toward the floor, hiding access to her mouth, it enraged Betty more than it should have. She threw the plate onto Alice's back, scalding her neck with the hot noodles.

Betty showed no sympathy when Alice cried out in pain. "I don't like this either," she said, pacing back and forth. "I can't let you go, but I can't have you starving to death either. At least not right now."

"Did — did you kill the other girls? Did you kill Sarah?" Alice asked with her voice trembling.

Betty stopped pacing. She squatted back down and grabbed Alice by the hair that grew from the nape of her skull, and lifted her head so she could get a better look at her face. With the grimy fork still in her hand, she shoved it into Alice's cheek, as if she were checking the tenderness of a steak. She pulled it back out, and dropped it to the floor, seeming to be shocked by her own actions. Her grip loosened from Alice's hair, and she stood up once more.

"I shouldn't have done that," she said, in absolute disbelief. Anger came over her just as quickly as the shock had, and she began kicking the walls. "Don't look at anything! Don't ask any questions! Just stay quiet, and mind your own business!"

Alice cried softly into the floor and tried to stay very still. Her heart beat with such intensity that it caused her body to ebb and flow involuntarily like a tide. She rocked herself into a dazed sort of stupor. Tiny beads of blood decorated her swollen cheek.

Something changed in Betty's demeanor again as she stared at the scene before her. Her moods and sanity were as inconsistent as Wintersburg's weather. Her knees grew weak, and she fell to the floor beside Alice. In a moment that seemed maternal, she began petting her head. Her voice became soft as if she were speaking to a small child.

"Why are you crying, sweetheart? Did my baby get hurt? Did you fall?"

Alice stayed silent.

"Sarah? Honey?" Betty continued. "Tell Mama what happened. I won't be mad. I promise."

Alice's vision went black once more, and she passed out with her head in Betty's lap. She spent her next days in and out of consciousness like this, with Betty visiting her, bringing her food, and forgetting reality for moments at a time. After a while, she completely stopped responding to the madness and ate the food as quietly and quickly as possible. She let Betty rant, panic, and dissolve into her safer memories, over and over again.

But, much like Betty's moods, things changed abruptly one day.

"Will would like to keep you inside

with him from now on. I have too many things to do, so I can't keep visiting you out here. Besides, it's only a matter of time before someone comes out to snoop around. Those deputies already brought their canines by here once. Fortunately, they thought the dogs were freaking out because I had the smoker going." she laughed lightly, and snorted even lighter. "They even stayed for a couple pulled pork sandwiches from the crockpot. Oh, if only they knew."

"Cook me dinner," Will said bluntly to Alice.

Betty stopped laughing and wiped her eyes. "Will, you know that's a bad idea. I'll make you something to eat instead," Betty said before turning back to Alice. "We're going to bring you inside and get you cleaned up a bit. There's a room in the basement. It should be better than the shed at least. I don't think it stinks as bad."

Will nodded to Alice, agreeing with Betty's statement. "It smells like Mama's things down there. You'll like it."

"You're right, Will. She'll like it a lot. Good then. Let's get going." Betty reached for Alice and lifted her arms into the air for Will to snip the ropes from them. She moved down to her ankles, and they were freed as well. "Damn... that's a really bad rope burn. It looks like it might be infected. Hmm... it's probably because you're covered in shit and piss. I guess that's my fault for not giving you a toilet, huh?" she laughed again as if she was delivering the punchline to some kind of a dark joke that only she understood.

Alice continued with her silence and obeyed the orders with a zombie-like state of emotional absence. She barely winced from the discomfort of her joints being used for the first time in days. Her face showed no expression as she walked, even though one of her ankles had started oozing and bleeding from the weight of each step. She was led all the way into the main bathroom.

When Betty failed to check the temperature of the water before pushing her into the shower, Alice showed no signs of resistance to the cold pouring down onto her flesh. She simply shook and waited for the next command.

"You'll do whatever Will wants. If he wants you to play dress up, you play dress up. If he wants you to be quiet, you sure as hell better be quiet. Don't worry though. He won't touch you. He's not a pervert."

Chapter 18

"Perfect Strangers"

Will walked down the stairs and into the basement of the lake house. It was filled with old decorations, broken Christmas trees, boxes of smashed ornaments, and expired canned goods, among other even less interesting things.

Anything that Betty couldn't bear to part with over the years had been shoved down there, to be stored indefinitely. She had intended on going through all of it and organizing everything, but other tasks had taken priority of her time. The last thing on her mind was where the Easter decorations or Valentine's Day cookie cutters from 1970 were.

Plywood shelves lined the painted brick walls and were absolutely covered with cobwebs and dust. Sticky ball canning jars were busted on the floor, with their lids rusted and warped. Dead and dried spiders littered the corners, forming a poorly knitted scarf of fibrous matter across anything that had been stacked nearby the walls.

While he was pushing webs out of his face, Will walked toward a small side room and shoved a long skeleton key into its lock. Once inside, he made his way over to an old creaky rocking chair. Its waxy finished showed its age from the years of sticky dark grime that had settled in between the pieces of wood that formed its shape. Decades of heavy use and improper cleaning had left the whole thing warped and discolored. A thin hand sewn cushion rested in the seat, tied by strings to the backing. Its floral pattern was yellowed, stained from nicotine, and partially moth-eaten. The entire room smelled like mildew and mothballs, but the bugs must have grown used to the repellent over the years because they'd clearly been feasting on all of the exposed fabrics.

He looked over to Alice. She was crumpled up like a ball of paper on the floor, bound again by her wrists. Her ankles remained free this time, so she was able to walk around the small space. It didn't look as if she had moved in a while though. Will had forced her to wear one of his mother's dresses, and she hadn't seemed to enjoy it. When she frowned, he had smacked her across the head.

She'd been resting in the corner ever since.

Will grinned and sat down carefully into the chair, with each creak of the weakened wood sending chills of pleasure up his body. He shuddered happily and leaned far back into it. Both of his palms rested onto the arms of the chair, and he rocked back and forth, gently. For several minutes, he stayed like that, moving rhythmically and slowly. But completely out of nowhere, he picked up speed. The chair started to rock violently, with Will's knees practically jumping from the floor for several seconds.

But, then he stopped just as abruptly.

His mother's voice filled the safe space in his mind, and he heard her speaking to him.

"William! You're going to break the damned thing if you keep treating it like that! Calm down, or I'm going to spank you good again!"

"Yes, Mama," He said out loud to the basement room.

"Now come here and give me some hugs. You know I hate yelling at you, boy."

Will lifted his arms and stood to his feet. He hugged the air, and then he hugged himself, too. "I love you, Mama," he said, before relaxing back into the chair.

More memories if his mother came to mind. He saw her combing through her dark hair, with small bald patches revealing themselves after each pass of the bristles.

***

The Lake House, 1985

Will had been noticing that his mother's head was becoming more and more bald with each treatment of chemo that she had been receiving. He didn't quite understand that the nurse had actually been trying to help, so when his mother yelped in pain during the poking and prodding of needles and other things, he had jumped up, and shoved the nurse down to the floor. That woman never came back to their home again, but Mrs. Noe didn't have more than two weeks left on the earth anyway.

Three nights before her passing, Will had sneaked into his mother's room to watch her from the closet, which was something that he did quite frequently. He enjoyed watching her sleep. Her small relaxed snores made him feel safe and calm as if nothing in the world was capable of hurting him.

Only, his mother didn't go to bed right away that night. Instead, she leaned forward, and removed a soft knitted cap, and placed it down beside her on the bed. She slowly lifted one of her hands to the side of her head and ran her fingertips across the bare and tender skin that covered her skull. With shaking bones, she picked up her hairbrush from the nightstand, and combed the air around her face, passing it through the ghosts of her brunette locks. Tears streamed down her cheeks and they fell into the dips of her collarbones — a place that was once tickled by the length of her hair.

Will understood her loss. He, too, missed brushing through every single strand that grew upon her head. She used to let him pin it all up in curls, poorly, but she wore them around with pride.

"What is going to happen to you when I'm no longer here to keep you safe?" she had once asked him.

He hadn't understood what she really meant by that question. Mothers didn't just leave their sons behind. "I'll be safe," he had replied. "You always find me when I get lost."

"That's not what I meant, my little bread loaf," she'd told him, through tear-shined eyes. "One day, and very soon, I won't be able to come home anymore —" She choked on her words momentarily and cupped Will's stubbly gray chin. "You're going to have to be strong for me, okay? Listen to your brother and sister. You need to be a good boy for me, Will."

He smiled. "Okay, Mama. You know I always behave."

"But, we know how you can get, sometimes," she'd said, with concern on her face. "You need to focus. I need you to try to stay present."

"I've been doing better."

***

After Will's mother had been in the earth for a few months, he still hadn't come to terms with her death. One September morning, he was making his usual rounds throughout the town, pulling his red wagon behind him. It had a few soda cans inside of it, but not much else. He left it outside and walked into Medley's. While he was standing in front of the bread section, his eyes caught sight of an attractive brown-haired woman. She looked nothing like his mother, but at that moment, she'd become a younger version of her to Will. He peeked at her through the stacks of loaves while she stood off in the distance, deciding on which type of chips she wanted to buy that day.

After she had picked up a bag, he followed her all the way over to the checkout and then waited for her outside of the store. As soon as she walked outside and went around the corner to go to her car, Will stepped out, directly in front of her, and caused a collision of their bodies.

He fell to the ground and started crying into the gravel.

"Oh my god! Are you okay?" She asked, panicked.

Will cried louder.

She crouched next to him and grabbed his hand. "Here, let me help you back up. Where does it hurt?"

Will stood up and walked to the bench by the bulletin board. He sat down and sobbed loudly into his palms. The woman sat beside him and patted him gently on the back.

"Your name's Will, right?" she asked. "My name is Jessica. Do you want me to drive you back to your house?"

Will nodded and looked at her through his fingers.

"Here, go hop in the car and I'll put your wagon in the back seat." She handed him the keys and bag of chips. "It's the black car right over there."

He climbed inside and sat patiently in the passenger's seat while she shoved the wagon behind him. A sly and satisfied smile formed across his face as he imagined everything that was about to happen. He was going to have his mother back again. He could prove the entire town wrong. *"She alive — she'd just been at Medley's the whole time."*

Jessica drove through the streets, anxious as to whether or not she'd seriously hurt him. He seemed fine though, and this eased her mind a little bit. She figured that Betty would be home, and she could just explain the situation to her. After all, how bad could that fall have even been? She'd hardly even felt herself bump into him.

"Alright, here we are," she said as they

pulled into his driveway. She followed it all the way behind the house and then put the car into park. "Is your sister home? Do you want me to go talk to her?"

"Yes, she's home. Come in," he said, nodding.

She took the wagon out of the car and pushed it next to the back porch, and then followed Will to the door. A feeling of dread came over her, but it was eased when she noticed the pretty paintings and the orderly home. It was a stark contrast to what it would eventually become.

Will pointed to the basement door. "She's down there," he said calmly.

"In the basement?" Jessica asked, confused.

"Yes. She's canning food."

"That's weird," she thought. *"You need the stove to can stuff. Maybe he meant that she's just putting the cans down in the pantry or something."*

"Oh, alright." She walked down the stairs, calling Betty's name out as she reached the bottom. There was no answer, so she called for her again, and walked into the small room to the side. There was nothing to see except for junk, a dresser, and a deteriorating rocking chair. "Betty? Are you down here? Will got hurt at Medley's today, and I —"

Thud

Will pushed her to the ground from behind and sat on her back to pin her down. She squirmed beneath him, and tried to turn herself over, or even to flip him off of her.

She was stuck.

"Get off of me!" she screamed, pushing up from the floor. "What the hell are you doing?"

"Sit still," Will sat calmly.

She fought even harder.

"Let me cut your hair!" he yelled, growing frantic and impatient. "I need it!" He held a pair of sewing scissors in his hand, presumably from the stack of quilting supplies that they'd passed by in the living room on their way downstairs.

"What?! Let me go!" she cried out, managing to push him over.

She climbed to her hands and knees, and then to her feet. Will grabbed her by the ankle and sank the scissors into her heel.

Jessica fell back to the ground, wincing in pain. "Please don't hurt me! Why are you doing this?"

Will climbed back on top of her, but he sat on her chest this time. He tried to move her hands underneath his legs too, but she was stronger than he had expected.

She reached up and clawed at his neck and chest, and then smacked him frantically.

"Sit still!" he yelled.

"Let me go!" she yelled back at him, over and over again.

"You need to be quiet! You're going to wake my sister!"

Jessica screamed as loud as she could. "Help me! Help! I'm down here! Help me!"

Will panicked and held his hands over her mouth and nose. She bit the meat of his palm, and he let go. He took his shirt off, receiving several scratches all along his bare torso, and then stuffed the fabric deep into her mouth. He pushed down as hard as he could until she stopped moving.

And then there was silence.

"There," he said. "You need to stay quiet like this."

He grabbed her hair and cut it all off, laying it onto the floor next to him carefully. When he was finished, he opened the dresser that had once been in his mother's room and rummaged around. He found her hairbrush in a shoebox and placed the bundle of hair in with it.

"I brought you something, Mama," he said. "Now you can feel pretty again. You don't have to cry anymore."

The room was very quiet, and Will sat down in the rocking chair. He rocked slowly, almost in a catatonic state for about an hour. Without warning, he stopped and looked at Jessica's body on the floor.

"Mama!" he yelped and repeated a similar phrase to the one that Jessica had used at Medley's. "Did you fall? Are you hurt?"

He stood up and lifted Jessica's body, placing it upright in the chair. "Why are you wearing shoes inside? I'll take them off for you." He removed her canvas slip-ons and tossed them into the dresser as well, next to the box. His eyes caught sight of a nightgown that his mother used to wear often, and he pulled it out. "Here. Let's make you more comfortable."

He took off Jessica's red jacket and threw it down as if it were nothing more than a piece of trash. He lifted her legs, and pulled the blue jeans off of her slumping body and tossed them to the floor as well. Carefully, he slid the nightgown over her body, pulling her arms through the lace-adorned sleeves. He positioned her to look more natural and comfortable, and then he stood behind the chair, rocking it, lovingly.

"There you go, Mama. You can sleep now. I know you are always so tired these days," he whispered.

Jessica's mouth fell open and revealed her swollen and bitten tongue. Will rocked her for a while until he heard Betty walking around upstairs.

She called out for him from above. "Will! Where did you run off to?"

He didn't answer.

She walked down the basement stairs and saw that the light was on in the side room. "Will, you can't keep messing around with mom's stuff. It's not good to dwell on sad things all the time. Come upstairs and help me figure out what to make for din —" She stopped and stared at the scene in front of her.

Will fell to the floor into the pile of Jessica's clothes and cried hysterically. Reality had set in the moment that his sister's fearful eyes had appeared, and he was terrified.

Betty cleaned up the mess and wheeled Jessica's body into the woods that night, using Will's red wagon to transport her. After failing to cut her up into smaller pieces to dispose of into the lake, she settled on a single shallow grave instead.

"I have to protect Will," she thought while flinging scoops of dirt behind herself with a shovel. *"He doesn't know any better. He isn't right."*

Betty sloppily dressed Jessica back into her coat and jeans, and rolled her into the hole. "There. Out of sight, out of mind."

The years passed by, leaving Ashley and Tammy to meet similar fates. Each time Will had attacked, he'd used sympathy to lure the girls somewhere secluded. He'd try to get more hair for his mother, and they would fight back, fearing the worst. If they hadn't screamed so loudly, they probably would have survived their encounters.

Will just couldn't handle the noise. It made him panic. It caused him to act out of instinct, and to suffocate each girl until they stopped clawing and crying.

Only after he sat in the rocking chair, would he find himself back in reality, realizing that each woman was an imposter — that his mother had been gone for a long time and that she wasn't ever coming back again. These moments would cause him to shriek uncontrollably, leaving Betty to clean up after him.

Unlike Jessica though, the others weren't left in lakeside graves.

Things were different with Sarah though. She had been there all along, within reach. Will loved her as if she were his other sister, instead of only loving her as if she were just his niece. He'd visit her on his trips around the town sometimes, and she'd feed him ice-cream, or treat him to pizza from Kirt's Pub. They were close, and they spent a lot of their free time together. He had even spent a few nights out bowling with her and Tiffany.

One day, Will had been feeling a little off. The boys in the town had spent the entire afternoon teasing him about Elvis and were begging him repeatedly to do impressions. When he finally caved in and gave them their show, they fell over, laughing hysterically. It took far too long for Will to realize that they were actually making fun of his performance, instead of just laughing along with enjoyment.

***

February 16th, 1988

Two months before Alice arrived

Will stood on the sidewalk, singing and dancing in front of a small crowd. The boys, all appearing younger than ten-years-old, laughed and mimicked his movements. They begged for more, buckling over as they watched Will thrust his body all around, singing loudly about hound dogs and tender loving. One of the boys even handed him a stick to use as a microphone. To Will, this was a great honor of encouragement. He belted his heart out onto the concrete, letting the boys stomp on it mercilessly. It didn't bleed, though, until the oldest of the group grew courageous and cold.

"No, don't do it," the youngest one mumbled.

"You should totally do it!" another one added, more loudly. He clasped his hands together with enthusiasm.

"Hey, Will," the oldest boy said. "I heard something the other day that you might like to hear."

Will stopped dancing and smiled really big. "What is it?" he asked, no longer singing.

"Elvis is dead."

"No, he's not!" Will cried out. "He's alive!"

"Nope. He's dead, just like your crazy

mom!"

Will shook with anger, and the boys took off running.

"Mama is alive!" Will yelled. "I'll prove it!" He yanked the handle of his wagon and wheeled it angrily through the streets.

He passed by his niece, Sarah, at her house, and she waved to him from the porch.

"Hey, Will, what's wrong, buddy?" she asked, noticing his tear-filled expression.

He froze.

"Come inside. I'll make you something warm to eat and we can watch some TV together."

Will turned and scooted his wagon into the grass. "Okay," he said, suddenly a little more calm.

He followed her inside. The smell of her coconut-scented perfume sparked a sudden curiosity about Sarah that he'd never felt before. He noticed the way her brown hair shined under the kitchen light, and it reminded him of his mother.

"I have to use the bathroom," he said, before walking down the hallway.

"That's fine. I'll heat up some raviolis for us."

Will shut himself in the bathroom,

making sure to leave it unlocked. He rummaged through the drawers under the mirror and found a pair of scissors that Sarah had often used to trim her bangs with between haircuts. While waiting for her to become worried and to go looking for him, he sat on the toilet and plotted.

When more time had passed by than he had expected, he picked up a bottle of shampoo from the shower and threw it to the ground. It landed loudly, and he screamed out in fake pain.

"Will! Are you okay? I'm coming in!" she called out while turning the handle on the doorknob.

Will moved himself down to the floor, and sat in a ball, waiting for her to get closer. She knelt down to put her arms around him. Once in a hug, he grabbed a handful of her long hair and started cutting it off.

Sarah grabbed his wrist and tried to pull away. "What are you doing? Put those down!" she said sternly, not realizing what was about to come her way.

"Sit still," Will replied.

He swung the scissors toward her head again, but she pushed him away and stood to her feet.

Will lifted the scissors into the air and pushed them into her thigh. When she buckled over, he very methodically pulled her the rest of the way to the floor and sat on her chest. He dropped the scissors, and she grabbed onto them.

Will wrapped his hands over her mouth and nose, and she dug the scissors into his side. They caught onto his shirt, but this absolutely enraged him, and he wrestled the blades from her hands. She screamed, and he brought them down over and over into her throat and face until the room was silent.

He resumed the haircut, sat it all onto the countertop, and then turned the shower on. Realizing that he'd made a huge mess, he thought it would be responsible to clean it all up before leaving. Over the course of a few hours, Will mopped and sopped, until both Sarah and the bathroom were clean, at least at first glance. He walked into the kitchen, grabbed a few black trash bags, and wrapped up the blood-drained body. Will waited until the sun went down completely and then dragged it out onto the porch, plopping it down into his wagon.

The slight trail that her body left on the concrete and in the grass was washed away later by the night's cold rain showers.

Will wheeled Sarah through the streets and all the way back to his house. He went inside to grab a flashlight and a shovel, before spending the entire night concealing the evidence of his crime. He used a small hand saw to remove enough of the floor in the shed, exposing the ground below. Fortunately for him, the dirt was soft and wet, which made it easier to clear out. Coldly, he tossed Sarah inside, trash bags and all, and covered her back up with shovels full of earth.

Seemingly without a care in the world, he went up to his bedroom, and fell asleep in his muddy clothes, as if nothing had even happened.

A day went by, and Betty became frightened. Usually, it was easy to reach Sarah. Her neighbor, Tiffany, hadn't seen her, and she hadn't shown up for her shift at the diner either. Betty walked upstairs to ask Will if he had talked to her recently, and she found him sitting up on the edge of his bed. He held onto Sarah's long hair, petting it, giggling while wearing a pair of shoes that she had bought for her the year before.

"Oh, God... What have you done?" Betty said, collapsing to her knees.

Will stopped giggling and dropped Sarah's hair in his lap. "She's in the shed. We can move her to the crawlspace. It's nice in there."

Chapter 19

"How Will I Know?"

Two days after Alice had first gone missing, Detective Darrow feared for the worst when she still hadn't answered any of his phone calls. He drove past her house, but he didn't see her car in the driveway. Hoping for the best, he figured that she might have just gone to the city to have a temporary change of scenery or something. When he arrived at the police station, he saw two other officers huddled, acting incredibly nervous and fidgety. He approached them, and stared at the desk that they had been leaning over. His eyes wandered to a stack of freshly printed flyers, and he reached for one. It took only a fraction of a second for him to realize that he was staring at a poorly photocopied photograph of Alice. He read the details listed below her picture, in complete disbelief of what was happening.

Missing

Alice Foster, aged 23 at the time of her disappearance, was last seen on November 15th, 1988, leaving Edna's Salon on Main Street. She is believed to have been wearing a pink sweater, a black skirt, and a pair of pink high-heeled shoes. Brown hair. Brown eyes. No known tattoos.

Detective Darrow's heart stopped for a moment. He felt as if he had just taken a bullet to the chest. A mixture of guilt and confusion erupted from his mind, and he started kicking the legs of the desk angrily. The other officers tried to calm him down, but he couldn't relax. He was determined to find out what had happened and was unwilling to sit around, taking phone calls or hanging flyers up at Medley's. There was no way that he was going to stay back and just wait for answers to come to him. He was going to find them, himself, even if it meant risking his own life in the process. Backup or not, he was going to bring Alice home again.

"Who reported this?" he asked the others.

"Edna Costa, her boss. I guess they called each other pretty religiously most nights when they would get home from the salon. When Alice didn't call her on Tuesday night, she figured that she was probably just busy. But, then Alice didn't show up for her shift yesterday either, so she stopped by to let us know. She seemed pretty worried."

"Call the Sheriff."

Detective Darrow darted back toward the door. He hopped in his patrol car and drove to the last place Alice had been seen — Edna's Salon. The entire building was constantly rich with gossip, so he figured that it would be a good place to start for multiple reasons. His wheels crunched against the gravel as he rolled in, driving faster than what was typical in the town. He had no time to waste. Every second was a second closer to something awful happening, if it hadn't already. He hurried inside, knocking the bell off of the door. It collapsed to the ground, sounding like glass shattering.

"Can I have everyone's attention?" he asked loudly. "Sorry for the interruption, but this is an emergency. As you all have heard, I'm sure, Alice Foster is missing. Edna here," he said, pointing beside him, "she let us know that Alice didn't show up for her last shift. Normally, we wouldn't be too concerned in such a short amount of time, but given the circumstances, all of us at the station are taking this very seriously. She can't be reached by phone, and no one has found her car. If anyone has any information at all, even something that doesn't really seem important, please let me know. The smallest detail could help us find her."

He looked around the room at the women. They all gossiped quietly to each other, with eyes big and bulging. They had so much to say, but just not to him. He stopped and focused on one elderly woman in particular who sat alone under a dryer. She had the hood lifted, and seemed very uncomfortable.

Every now and then, she glanced over from the sides of her eyes to Detective Darrow, appearing like a child who knew they were guilty of something. He walked over to her and sat in the empty seat beside her.

"Do you know something, Ma'am?" he asked, quietly. "Anything at all?"

She shifted in her seat and whispered, "I might, but I swore I wouldn't tell. It might get her in trouble. I can't be responsible for that."

Detective Darrow nodded. "Well, what's worse, ma'am — getting her in a little bit of trouble, or risking her life?"

The woman gasped, seeming appalled at the suggestion, but then she pursed her lips. "You're right," she said, shaking her head. "Just don't mention that I was the one to tell you. I don't need any of these loonies talking about me too."

"That's fine. I won't say a word. Just tell me. What do you know?"

She cupped her hand to Detective Darrow's ear. "She's been doing Betty's hair over at her house on the lake."

He turned to look at her for a moment. "What's the problem with that?" he asked, confused.

"She stole a client from the salon. Edna can't make money off of that, so she could get fired. It's a big deal to go to clients' houses. I thought that was obvious," she continued to whisper, more loudly this time.

Detective Darrow understood. "Is that

all you know?" he asked.

"I know she was supposed to do her hair there on Tuesday night. She went over there most Tuesdays, actually. I saw her packing up Betty's orange rollers when I stopped by to pick up a new bottle of shampoo before they closed that night."

His face went pale, and he patted the woman on the back, lightly. "Thanks so much, Ma'am. I'll head over there right away. And don't worry. I'll keep it a secret."

She nodded and opened a magazine, trying to look preoccupied.

Detective Darrow walked back to the front of the salon and slammed a stack of flyers onto the receptionist's desk. "If you all have some time, pass these around. If you hear anything at all, call the station. You can be anonymous if you wish. Thanks for your time, ladies."

He waved to Edna, and smiled courteously to everyone else, before walking back out to his car.

"Hopefully Betty knows something," he thought as he started the engine. *"She's my only lead right now."*

***

Detective Darrow pulled into the driveway. Nothing seemed out of place, and Betty's car was in the driveway. He saw Will's wagon pushed up against the porch. His stomach churned from anxiousness as he approached the back door. Lifting a hand in the air, he made a fist and knocked several times. There was shuffling inside, and he heard Betty mumbling to herself as she got closer.

She turned the handle and stood before him in complete disarray. Her hair was a mess as if she'd fallen asleep with it wet, like it had been styled by a mix of the pillow and her bad dreams. She wore a tattered over-sized men's shirt and loose gray sweatpants. Her feet were bare and covered only by bruises and small scabby cuts.

"Yeah, what do you need officer?" she asked, appearing both confident and annoyed by his presence.

"Do you have a minute to talk? It's very important," he asked, stepping forward.

She looked behind herself at the mess that she called home and shrugged. "I haven't cleaned in a while, but you can come in, I guess. What's so important that you need to talk at this hour?"

"Is the morning not good for you, Mrs. Noe? I didn't think it was too early. I apologize if I'm interrupting anything." He spoke with the polite tone that the older generation appreciated.

She waved a weak finger in front of her face and motioned for him to sit down on the couch the way that someone would instruct a dog.

He sat down, and leaned forward, unable to get comfortable. All around, he saw trash bags and wine bottles. The house was a complete mess, bordering on a health hazard. Judging her living conditions wasn't important at the moment though, so he tried to ignore the food odors and the mountains of garbage. Even though it was cold outside, there were still a few flies lingering around.

"I guess I didn't realize the time. Anyway, your reason for coming here is...?"

He could tell she wasn't fond of his company and was growing more and more impatient the longer he acclimated to the house.

"You know Alice Foster, correct?" he asked, cutting right to the chase.

"Yeah, I know her. What about her?"

"She never showed up for yesterday's shift, or for today's either. She has been declared a missing person by our police department. Here, let me hand you a flyer." He reached into his jacket, and unfolded a piece of paper, handing it to her.

She grabbed it, showing little interest, and held it out in front of her. "That's not good at all. But, why did you come all the way over here to tell me about it?"

"Well," he said, clearing his throat and sitting up more straight. "I heard that she comes over here on Tuesdays to do your hair sometimes. Seeing that she went missing on Tuesday, I figured I'd stop by to see if you've heard anything, or if you might have seen her that night. I'm trying to piece every last detail together to find out if anything can lead us to her somehow."

Betty paced back and forth a couple of times, and raised her hands above her head. She was nervous, but she could have passed as having been concerned for Alice.

"She never stopped by," she said, with a matter-of-fact tone. "I mean, look at me. Is this the hair of someone who had a professional do it? Not at all. I ended up washing my own hair last night, and never got around to styling it. I figured she just got busy or something and didn't show up. You know how young people are. They don't think to call. I know her friend recently died too, so I assumed she might've just been a little depressed or something. God knows I can definitely relate to that feeling."

Detective Darrow nodded and scanned the room one more time. While the place was disgusting, nothing really raised any red flags for him. Betty definitely hadn't gotten her hair done the night before, so it seemed likely that Alice really had never made it over to the house. He wondered where had she actually gone after work then.

"Alright," he said, standing to his feet. "Please, let me know if you hear something."

"You know I will. I really hope she's okay."

"Oh, and Mrs. Noe —"

"M-hmm?"

"We're doing everything we can to find Sarah, too. I don't want you thinking that we just gave up on her. I know you're bitter toward all of us. The whole town is growing impatient actually, but just understand that we're doing everything possible to bring her home, too."

"Thanks. I needed to hear that," she said, with insincerity in her heart.

"Yep. Alright. I'll get out of here, then. Have a good day, Ma'am."

He nodded and stepped outside.

***

That night, to celebrate narrowly escaping a surprise visit from Detective Darrow, Betty decided that there would be a family dance party in the living room. She spent a decent amount of time pushing all of the furniture and bags of trash against one of the walls or shoving them into the kitchen. The only things that remained in the living room were the stereo and a small table for drinks and chips.

"Will!" she yelled down the basement stairs. "Get Alice dressed, and put on one of your ties. We're going to have a party!"

"A party!" he yelled back excitedly from his mother's rocking chair. "Okay, give me a few minutes and we'll be right up!"

"Don't take too long, okay? The chips are almost stale already."

Will rummaged in the drawers and piles for a suitable dress for Alice. He found one of his mother's favorites and untied Alice's wrists. He knew that she was too weak to fight back if she wanted to anyway. He shoved the dress into her lap and gave her an encouraging smile before his attention turned to a pair of shoes.

"Here. Wear these too. Mama wore these at the funeral."

"Funeral?" she asked. Her voice was weak, and she didn't really want an explanation as to how he had acquired them. She'd just been surprised by his statement.

"That's what I said. Hurry up. We have things to do."

Alice slipped the dress over her shoulders, and slid the previous one down her waist, letting it fall to the floor. Judy's clothes were a few sizes too big for her, so it made them easy to put on and to remove. That was the only benefit of having to wear them.

Will slid each shoe onto her feet and helped her up. "There. Just like Mama." He led her up the stairs, ignoring her sharp groans of pain as the infected cut on her ankle ripped open a little more. Had he known that she had started to bleed onto his beloved shoes, he might have considered paying more attention to the situation.

"Here she is," Will said, moving behind Alice. "Doesn't she look beautiful?"

Betty made a sour face and rolled her eyes. "I always hated that dress. She can play with you later. Let's have Sarah come back for the night. Would that be okay?"

Will pouted and looked down at the floor. "Fine."

"Let me get her some different clothes, and I'll be right back," she said, while she headed upstairs. "And come put on your tie like I said."

Will nodded and followed her up the stairs.

Within an hour, they were dressed like they were about to go to a hillbilly ball. Music filled the air, along with the occasional scent of garbage or wine. Will stood next to the stereo, singing an Elvis song, while Betty sang into her glass bottle. Alice stood in the corner, wearing one of Sarah's dresses, with Judy's shoes still on her feet.

Betty walked over and put her arms underneath Alice's, forcing her sick-and-slumping body to dance along with her. She wobbled Alice across the floor like she was a water-logged Raggedy Anne doll, trying to mimic a dance as best as she could.

"Isn't this fun, Sarah?" she asked. "Remember when we used to dance together all the time?"

Alice nodded to appease her. She knew that it would be easier to just go along with the delusions. Resisting only caused more problems. She was aware that Betty was unable to admit any of her faults. Any questioning or correcting seemed to lead the strange woman to feel attacked, which never ended well for anyone.

"Sing for us. I haven't heard you sing in so long," Betty suggested.

"I — I can't," Alice replied, with her voice weak and scratchy.

Betty stopped moving her around and dropped her hands down to her side. She watched as Alice collapsed onto the floor right in front of her. All of the excitement and life drained from her expression, and there was no empathy in her eyes. "What do you mean you can't?" she asked with a voice as cold as winter.

"I don't feel well. My throat hurts."

"Why does your throat hurt, Sarah?" Betty asked, putting her hands onto her hips. She leaned forward a little as if she were trying to see Alice a little better.

"I don't know. It just —"

"You're ruining everything right now. Did you really think that I'd believe you were Sarah? You're an imposter. Why are you trying to trick us?"

"I'm not trying to trick you!" Alice cried out, her voice cracking on the last word.

"Will! Take this lunatic back down to the basement. I won't stand by and let someone toy with our emotions like this in our own home. Do what you want with her. She'll be meat by the weekend anyway."

"But, Betty," Will tried to understand. "I thought we were just playing. We can still dance without her."

"No. Get her out of my face or I'm going to absolutely lose my mind."

Will pouted and led Alice down the stairs. While he was used to Betty's mood swings, he had been hoping to have a good time. He felt extremely disappointed, but he didn't blame Alice, fortunately. He sat her down in the corner of the side room, bound her hands once more, and locked her inside.

***

Detective Darrow had a bad feeling the entire night. He didn't feel as if he had looked around the property enough while he was at Betty's. When the morning came, he drove back to her house, planning on asking her a few more questions. At the very least, he figured that she might know where else he could look. Without her, he was at a dead end.

Right when he was about to open the driver's side door to step out, he noticed Will sitting down by the shed. He hadn't seen Will in a while, but he always liked him well enough. Remembering that he was always out walking around, Detective Darrow figured that it wouldn't hurt to see if he knew anything about Alice. He walked down toward the lake, hoping for the best. Will sat, staring down at his feet, giggling and whispering. Detective Darrow looked down to see what was so amusing and noticed that Will was wearing a pair of hot pink high heels. His feet were crammed inside of them, causing the leather to bulge out. His smaller toes were hanging out of the top, off to the side, unable to be squeezed into the pointed tip. Detective Darrow recognized them as Alice's. They were one of her favorite pairs. She wore them to work most days.

"Will?" he asked, sternly. "Where did you get those shoes?"

Will looked up at him and stopped giggling. His expression went from amused to frightened, and he stood up. He fell back down, unable to balance in the small heels.

"Will. I asked where you found those shoes. Those are Alice Foster's, am I right?"

He took one of them off and threw it at Detective Darrow's head, missing it, barely. He kicked the other shoe off, leaving it to fall into the mud, and ran back up toward the house.

Detective Darrow chased after him and ran in through the back door. He chased Will all the way to the basement steps, just as Betty was reaching the top of them. She had gone downstairs to make sure Alice was still locked in the small basement room.

Will plummeted into Betty like a football player, knocking her down the steep wooden steps. She crashed into the concrete floor and immediately went limp. Blood pooled out from behind her head, but Will hopped over her as if she were nothing more than a dish that he'd dropped. He fumbled with his keys and unlocked the side room, before shutting himself inside with Alice. There was no way to lock the door from the inside, but he didn't consider any of the risks at that moment. To him, he wasn't hiding Alice in the basement — he was running to his mother. He fell down beside her, grabbed onto her, and buried his face into her chest for safety.

He pulled away and stood back to his feet, pacing back and forth, mumbling to himself. In a matter of seconds, he started smacking his face over and over and sank down into the rocking chair. In a desperate attempt to trance out into an even safer mental space, he rocked rapidly and hummed his favorite song.

Detective Darrow burst into the room and saw Alice's thin body curled into a ball on the floor next to the completely mentally absent Will. Without even blinking, he reached for his radio and called for backup.

He hadn't expected to find her so quickly.

Chapter 20

"Trading Places"

The hospital was cold. No matter how many of those thick cotton blankets the nurses stacked on top of her, Alice's bones still shook from beneath them. She hated spending her days and nights under what seemed like constant supervision. The bright lights made her feel exposed. She felt as if she were a zoo animal, on display for anyone who passed by to poke with needles, and to wheel her off into a new exhibit whenever they felt that it was necessary for her to have a change of scenery.

Detective Darrow visited as often as he could. Compared to any other faces that Alice had been seeing, he seemed to be as present as the seemingly permanent friction burns on her skin. They didn't look like they would be going away anytime soon, and neither did he. He treated Alice with care as if they'd known each other for many years. When she'd fall asleep throughout the day, which was actually fairly often, he would grab her hand in his, and let her squeeze the life out of it during the nightmares. He'd assist the nurses when her bandages needed to be changed, unwrapping her wrists like two fragile gifts. When she'd wince in pain as the infection was being cleaned out of them, he felt it too. Alice's wounds became his scars, and his burden to bear. Guilt wrapped itself around his neck, much like a rope, and he hung his head.

"If I had only kept a close eye on her, none of this would have happened," he kept thinking. *"If I had only been able to piece everything together sooner, she wouldn't have to be in this place right now."*

He had already taken initiative and left

a key behind for Edna. Together, they had intended on making sure that the refrigerator would be nicely stocked, and that everything would be clean and ready for Alice for when she was discharged from the hospital. They had wanted to make sure that all she needed to focus on was feeling better. Edna made her an assortment of soups and side dishes and stacked them orderly in plastic containers. Between those, and the various juices, Alice's fridge had been filled quickly.

Detective Darrow still had to work though. It was more important than ever, actually. Even though he typically had weekends off, he worked through them to make sure every loose end was tied, finally with the help of the Sheriff. He didn't want to give Will time to fabricate stories while Betty was healing, so he refused to sit at home or accept much downtime other than to visit Alice. He visited her often, but during the hours that he was gone from the hospital, she was left alone to squirm uncomfortably while her brain took her back to the shed over and over again.

One of the rope burns on Alice's ankles had gotten badly infected and caused her to have a sudden and high fever on her second night in the hospital. During these sweat-covered hours, she slept even more than before. In her waking moments, she watched the scrubs and white jackets go in and out of the room. Her mind was too foggy to be able to tell if it was a single nurse or doctor visiting frequently, or if it was multiple caretakers. In one instance, she even thought that one of the women had been her grandmother stopping by to console her.

"Alice," the older woman had said with a softness in her tone, "You need to get better soon, okay? We're all rooting for you."

"Grandma," she replied. "Please don't leave me again."

The nurse smiled and wiped a few damp strands away from Alice's forehead. "I'll stay with you. I'll be right here if you need anything. Now, let's get this fever lowered, okay?"

Alice nodded and drifted off into more peaceful dreams than before.

***

After a few more days, Alice was prepared to go back home. Her fever had gone away completely, and her wounds seemed to be on their way to healing properly. Once she'd been given the go-ahead from one of the hospital's physicians, she was free to resume life as it had been prior to any of this happening. There was something strange about being let loose like that, especially after such trauma — both physical, as well as emotional.

As she signed herself out, she wondered what she was even supposed to do next. Was she just supposed to go back home, and start working right away again? Was she supposed to take time off? Was this the reason that people spent their days and nights alone at the bars? She considered that maybe the bottles of liquor were a decent replacement for the IV fluids that she'd become accustomed to receiving through her bruised veins. She had no intentions of taking that bottomless route, though.

Detective Darrow showed up to take her home. He helped her into his car, and drove her back into town, unable to think of much to say during the drive. Each time he looked down at her bandages or looked up to see the large stab marks on her purple cheek, his heart ached. It hurt to see her in that condition. Through it all, though, he was just relieved that she was still alive. Compared to the other women, she'd been extremely lucky.

During the time that he had spent piecing the case together, he had discovered some really disturbing things. Will, while not intending on becoming a murderer, had kept a very large collection of trophies from his crimes. Seeing that his main motive for killing the women had been solely to retrieve the items, this came as no surprise to Detective Darrow. Still, it was an incredibly disturbing thing to sort through.

Will had kept a shoebox in the basement, hidden inside of his mother's old dresser. Betty had placed all of their mother's old items down there for safekeeping, but more so to keep herself from thinking about the loss as often. She figured that she and Will would have been able to move on more easily if the constant reminders were out of sight, but her plan hadn't exactly worked. Instead, she had unintentionally created a mausoleum, and her brother crept through its corridors, searching for signs of life among the moth-eaten quilts and scraps of death.

Inside of the shoe box, Will had kept piles of poorly chopped hair. Blood had dried on the ends of some, and the varying shades of brunette cuddled together for warmth inside of their unified cardboard grave. They had been a gift for his mother, but she no longer had the hands to receive it, or the scalp to wear it anymore. Many nights were spent with him rubbing handfuls of the Prell and hairspray scented strands to his face, inhaling deeply.

He had kept a smaller ponytail tied

together on the very top of the pile. It was Sarah's, and it resembled his mother's hair color and texture the most closely. Some nights, he would take it up to his bedroom. While there, he would pull out his mother's hairbrush to comb through the bundle, all while Elvis songs would play over the stereo in the background.

Aside from the hair, Will had kept a drawer full of shoes. While Detective Darrow hadn't noticed the importance at first, Jessica's body had been barefoot when found. Her shoes, Ashley's, and Tammy's were found among the collection, along with several pairs of Sarah's. Will had tried to wear a few of them, but judging from the stretching and tearing on some of the pairs, it was apparent that he had favored the bright colored high heels the most.

When Detective Darrow had taken him in for questioning, he had sat a few of the pairs on the table between himself and Will. He watched as Will shifted around uncomfortably in the chair, trying to look away.

Will's eyes would peek back over to the pile though, no matter how far or in what direction he turned his head. He just couldn't resist. Something drew him in, and it was beyond just the memories of his mother.

"Will," Detective Darrow said with seriousness in his voice. "Tell me about the shoes. Why did you keep them?"

"They're pretty." He was calm, and his words were blunt at first.

"Yes, they are, but a lot of things are pretty, some things are even prettier than these." He picked up one of Alice's pink high heels and flipped it around in his hand. He leaned forward across the table and sat it down, only inches away from Will. "I saw you wearing this pair. Do you remember?"

Will nodded. "I remember."

"Why were you wearing them? They don't seem to be your size." He picked up the matching pink shoe and moved it along the table. It made little knocking sounds as he mimicked the movements of footsteps. "Is it the noise that they make when you walk in them? Is this what you like?" he asked.

"No," Will said, maintaining his calmness. "It's not that."

"Then what is it? You can tell me. I'm not here to judge you, you know. I just want to know what was so special about them. I mean, I hear ya. They do look really nice. Actually, I might even want to try one on myself." He removed one of his own shoes and stood next to Will. He slipped the pink pump on, with only part of his foot able to fit inside, and he walked back and forth across the floor. "Oh wow. They feel nice too. I think I'm going to have to keep this pair for myself."

Will trembled and his face turned red. "Take them off," he said through clenched teeth. "Give them back. They're mine, not yours."

Detective Darrow took a mental note of Will's sudden switch in moods. He was finally getting under his skin. "Fine. You're right," he said, trying to look defeated. "I'll let you wear them for a minute, but you can't tell anyone about it. Promise?"

Will's anger settled down, and he looked surprised. "Really? I can do that?"

Detective Darrow nodded. "You have to be fast though, alright? I could get in trouble for letting you."

"Okay. I'll be quick."

Detective Darrow took Will's shoes off for him and slid each of the pink high-heels onto his large feet.

Will felt like Cinderella for a moment, as if he were receiving his missing glass slipper. The only difference was that the shoes were torn and covered in mud, and Will's feet didn't fit inside of them at all. He crammed his toes in as far as they would go, and then he sighed loudly, like someone lowering themselves into a hot bath on a cold day. He went silent after that for several seconds and then smacked his feet together.

"There's no place like home," he said. "I used to love watching that movie when I was your age. Have you seen the Wizard of Oz?"

"I have, but Will," Detective Darrow said. "You are my age. You have maybe five years on me, tops."

"Will? What do you mean?" Will replied in a high pitched voice. He looked extremely confused all of a sudden. "That's my son's name."

"Oh, I'm sorry. Could you tell me your name then? I seem to have forgotten it somehow."

Will smiled largely, something that was uncommon for him to do — even more uncommon than these bursts of talkativeness. "I'm Judy, silly. Judy Noe."

That was Will's mother's name. Detective Darrow realized what was happening and asked him more questions, hoping to see inside of his mind a little better. "Oh, you're right," he said, smacking himself lightly on the forehead. "Mrs. Noe. I can't believe I forgot that. Could you tell me where you came upon such beautiful pink shoes, Judy?"

Will's smile grew even larger. "My youngest son bought them for me."

Detective Darrow decided to see just how deep this wound was. He stepped back from Will and gasped. "But Judy! You look different. Where did all of your hair go?"

Will looked terrified in that a moment. He lifted his cuffed hands to his head and rubbed one of his forearms across his balding fine hair. His mother's exposed scalp came to mind, and he completely imploded.

"My hair!" he screamed, falling out of the seat and onto the floor. The high heels flew off of his feet upon impact. "What did you do with my hair?"

Detective Darrow crouched down beside Will to stabilize him, mostly to keep him from thrashing too hard and injuring himself. "Will, I need you to calm down and tell me why you kept a box of hair in the basement."

"My hair!" he screamed again. "I need to give it to Mama!" Will sobbed for several minutes until a wave of calmness settled over him.

Detective Darrow patted him on the back and lifted him back into his chair. "Did you cut it from those women?" he asked.

Will nodded and stared at the table.

"Did you mean to hurt them, or did you just want to help your mom?" he asked, trying to figure out the motive.

"I didn't want to hurt them, but they screamed."

"So, you didn't like the sound?"

Will shook his head again. "I hated it."

Detective Darrow saw the situation with a little more understanding and clarity. Perhaps Will wasn't as evil as he had initially thought. It seemed like he genuinely thought that he was aiding his dead mother.

Will had escaped into the shoes that he knew his mother would have loved, and he brought her back to life in the only way he knew how. During his moments when he'd pretend to be his mother, he was able to accept the gifts, and give himself words of approval. While some monsters are born, others are created. But, the worst monsters are those who believe themselves to be heroes. Will hadn't meant to be the villain. He just happened to become one along the way.

"Detective," Will said, suddenly. "There's something else."

"What is it? I'm all ears."

"That boy didn't kill the redhead."

Shock spread over Detective Darrow's

face. "Then who did? Was it you?"

Will nodded. "I didn't want to. I followed them home, but the other girl was gone when I knocked."

"So, Tiffany let you in?" he asked.

"She opened the door, and I walked in. She told me to get out, but I wanted her shoes."

Detective Darrow remembered Tiffany's decorated red heels from the crime scene. "You didn't take them though. What happened?"

"She screamed like the others," he said while staring off into a corner. "I was scared."

"So you killed her too?"

"She was too loud. I followed her into a bedroom, but she kept screaming. Then I heard someone at the door."

Detective Darrow leaned forward. "So you left before you could take them?"

"I went out of the window."

While all of this made sense, a confused feeling washed over him as he thought about Alice's encounter with Benji. While Benji was apparently innocent of Tiffany's death and of the other murders, he was still guilty of attempting a different one. Solving the case should have eased Detective

Darrow's mind, but he still felt very uneasy, as if something else was still looming nearby.

It didn't feel like it was over yet.

Chapter 21

"Family Ties"

June 14th, 1986

The cemetery welcomed Will through its creaking iron gates. He was a familiar face among the dead — possibly even more familiar than their own still-living friends and family members. People didn't typically enjoy walking past all of the tombstones, especially not on a regular basis. Death became too much of a reality during those times. Unfortunately, many graves were left untended and in shambles due to avoidance. Others, even less lucky, had their names eroded away and sun-bleached from their stones. Because of this, their caskets were left to become nothing more than occupied spaces. Their stories would never be told again. Their secrets were going to stay hidden in the grooves of their bones.

Judy Noe's grave was properly maintained and even beautifully decorated. Unfortunately, her body had been removed long before, while her flesh was still very much intact. This was before the mound of disturbed dirt could settle in place upon her casket. Will stopped by only to treat her gravesite as something that needed to be kept attractive. It was more of a bush that he enjoyed pruning and showing off than anything else. His mother's little plot of grass needed to be the most beautiful of them all. He wanted the other women, the ones who were once her peers, and the ones who would one day become neighbors to her tombstone, to be impressed by the sight of her — or just simply, to be impressed by her site.

This Saturday was different though. Will had noticed a young woman jogging through the narrow blacktop pathways. She had a friend with her, but that friend left after only a short while. The woman stopped to slump against the base of a tree. Will watched from behind a tall memorial statue as she drank speedily from a dripping water bottle. Sweat glistened across her skin, basting her in salt and oils like a Thanksgiving turkey.

Will's mouth salivated while he imagined the scent of her hair. Drool stretched down his lips and chin, and onto his shirt. He didn't bother to wipe it away as he approached her. He scrunched his face up to appear as if he was crying and added a few loud snorts and sniffling sounds to appear more convincing.

The woman climbed to her feet when she saw him. "What's wrong? Are you okay?" she asked, showing him sympathy.

Will cried even louder, adding in a few long and drawn out whines.

She patted his back. "Let me sit and talk with you. My name's Ashley. Can you tell me what yours is?"

He lowered his hands from his soaked face and looked up at her. Without needing to say anything, she knew his identity once she'd seen his eyes.

"Oh, I know you — you're Betty's

brother. Do you want me to walk you home?"

"That would be nice," he said, no longer crying.

"We can talk along the way if you'd like," she suggested.

Will nodded.

The cemetery wasn't far from the lake house. By foot, it was less than a five-minute walk. The people of Wintersburg had preferred to have that reminder of mortality on the edge of town, somewhere that they wouldn't have to see it all the time. They had abandoned their dead and blamed the bodies for no longer being alive.

Will didn't say much at all during their walk, but Ashley didn't pressure him to hold a conversation. Instead, she just commented on the weather and told him about how she would get sad too sometimes — that it was nothing for him to be ashamed of experiencing. He stared either ahead or down at his shoes, trying to decide what his next move would be. Betty wasn't home, but he was still hoping that Ashley would be quiet.

When they approached the house, he led her down to the shed near the water. "Will you help me for a minute?" he asked.

"I — I guess so," she replied as she followed him. She felt a lump in her throat like she was unable to swallow her saliva properly. Something didn't seem right, but she didn't question the feeling.

"I need help lifting something out of the shed. It's not heavy, but it's too big."

"Yeah, that's fine. I have to hurry though. I'm supposed to meet back up with my friend for dinner. I don't know if you saw her with me earlier or not. She just ran home to get a change of clothes first."

"It won't take long."

"What's that awful smell?" she asked covering her nose with the inside of her arm.

"A deer died in the woods."

She looked confused, but it didn't seem improbable.

Will opened the shed door and stepped to the side. It was too dark to see anything, and the odor in the air grew extremely foul. Flies darted out, and swarmed all around their heads, buzzing angrily.

"What the hell? Did you put the deer in there or something?" she said with concern in her voice.

Will had already grabbed the gardening shears from beside the shed door while Ashley had been batting away at the flies. He pushed her into the doorway and grabbed her by her ponytail. Immediately and methodically, he started chopping through her thick brown strands. She flailed and grabbed the back of her head out of instinct. The dirty shears sliced two of her fingers open, and she yelped in pain.

"You need to be quiet," Will said. There was no emotion in his voice.

"Get off of me, you creep!"

Will brought the sheers high into the air and shoved them deep into the back of her neck. He pulled them out, but with much less speed. They had wedged themselves in the space directly below her occipital bone, severing the connection between her head and spine.

She collapsed to the shed floor.

"There. That's better, isn't it Mama?" Will looked over to a large muddy suitcase in the back of the shed. His mother's portable grave stared back at him, with only darkness for eyes. He cut the rest of Ashley's hair and took it down to the basement, before returning to the shed once more. "I'm going to move you back home today. I already made a new spot for you. Are you ready?"

There was no answer.

"Okay, let's go," he said, suddenly happier. He pushed and pulled the suitcase and moved it back up to the house. Carefully, he pulled it toward the basement steps, and then shoved it gently down them. The suitcase bounced loudly until it hit the bottom with a loud thud. "There. You will like this better than the woods. I can visit you every day."

He brought down his shovel and a flashlight and walked to the space beneath the wooden stairs. There was a small rickety door that led into a spider-infested crawl space. He opened it and crouched inside, pulling the suitcase along with him. He clicked the flashlight on and pushed the suitcase into a large hole that he had dug in the dirt floor. He shoveled the piles of dirt back into place and concealed the grave before returning to the shed.

Ashley's body rested on the floor, but with only a small amount of blood staining the wood.

Will lifted her shorn head and pinched her cheeks as if he was trying to wake her from a deep sleep. "You can go home now," he said, smacking her lightly.

"Will!" Betty's voice called out from the driveway. "Will, where are you?"

"Oh no..." he muttered, realizing that his sister was going to know that he had made another mistake. "I have to hide. I need to hide." He scurried out of the shed like a scared mouse and headed into the safety of the woods.

Betty reached the shed and noticed the smell. Will had already explained to her, too, that a deer had died. She knew better than that though, but she didn't want to ask what he had really been up to. She pushed the shed door back open and saw Ashley's still-warm body.

"Dammit. Will! Get over here you son of a bitch!"

He peeked out from behind a tree and then sulked back over to the shed. "I didn't mean to do it. I swear. I think she fell."

"I can't keep doing this. It's killing me, Will. You need to get ahold of yourself."

"I'll try harder," he said. "I promise."

"Good..." she rubbed her head with disbelief. "Now go get that wagon and bring me your shovel."

Will headed to the back porch and grabbed the handle of his wagon. Just as he began rolling it down the hill, he heard someone pulling into the driveway. The car parked next to Betty's.

"Hi there, Will. Do you know where Betty is? I really need to talk to her. It's urgent," the elderly woman asked. She was thin and freckled, with bright white hair.

Will froze for a second, and darted down the hill with his wagon, not saying a word. The woman followed him, in fairly good condition for her age. She reached him only a short moment after he had stopped in front of the shed.

"Betty? Are you down here too?" she asked, moving in front of the doorway. "Betty? Will? Are you — Oh my —" she stepped back and tripped into the mud.

"Susan? Dammit. Can this day get any worse?" Betty replied, staring at her with surprise. "Don't scream. Don't say a thing. Just let me explain real quick."

Susan Foster pointed her thin finger at the body that rested only feet away from her. "But, the — what is tha — what is —" she stammered, unable to form her thoughts into sentences.

"Will, help me lead her back up the hill real quick."

With Susan's arms resting on each of their shoulders, they helped her up to the back porch, and into the house. Will dropped her onto the couch.

"Thanks, now go back outside. I need to talk to her alone, okay?"

Will nodded and left the house.

After several minutes of calming Susan down and easing her back into reality, Betty was able to start explaining things a little better. "I know what you saw is probably really scary right now, but you need to listen to me, okay?"

Susan nodded with her eyes wide and bloodshot.

"Will has a bit of a problem right now. I don't really know what's going on, but I can't let anything happen to him. You need to promise me that you'll keep what you saw a secret. Can you do that for me? Please? I'm begging you."

Several words finally managed to escape from Susan's mouth. "Betty. Dear. I've kept so many of your secrets over the years. How many more are you going to ask me to keep?"

Betty slapped her knee and leaned back into the chair across from Susan. "Are you really going to bring that up right now?"

"For over twenty years, I've been bearing your burdens. From the moment you slept with my son, like some kind of a stray cat. I even kept your pregnancy a secret. I lied to my boy for you."

"Just stop. We don't need to talk about this right now," Betty said in an irritated tone.

"Then when are we going to talk about it? Sarah doesn't know that she has a sister, and poor Alice — my sweet Alice thinks she's a damned orphan. If only she knew that her mother was just too ashamed to have kept her around. You know what I think is the sickest part of all of this?"

Betty crossed her arms and scowled.

"Betty, just listen to me for once. The sickest thing to me is that you went on to marry my son after trying out a few more guys in town first. Then when you had Sarah, you still didn't want to admit to anyone that you had another daughter before her. My son might have hated and avoided me for many reasons, but if he had known that I'd been keeping his own child from him, well, he might've had that stroke a lot sooner."

"So, I'm a piece of shit. What else do you want me to say? I abandoned my own child and chose to raise another one. Alice is doing great though, or am I wrong about that too?"

"I've loved her with every drop of blood in my body. And you're right. She's doing just fine without you. She's probably better off thinking that her real mother's dead."

Those last words cut Betty like a knife. She had always felt guilty for giving her first daughter away like she was nothing more than an old t-shirt, but she'd still felt the need to stay strong and committed to her decision. She prided herself on good values.

How would people have reacted if they'd known that she had a child out of wedlock in such a small gossip-filled town? What would people say if she had taken Alice back after she'd married Susan's son — if she'd just suddenly announced that she had abandoned her? Guilt was hard, but admission was harder.

"Susan. Please. Can't we stop this?"

"Do you have any idea how it feels for Sarah to not even know that I'm her grandma? I'm so tired of pretending to be some family friend. She hugs me like a friend. She thanks me like a friend. I've never gotten to hold one of my own grandbabies in my lap, and now she's all grown up. It's too late to ever get those moments back."

A sudden burst of aggression filled Betty. "Do you know what it's like, Susan? Do you have any clue how it feels to hide a pregnancy and to have to hand your baby off to someone else? Do you know how it feels to stay up all night long for years, wondering if your child is hurt or crying, or if they've been eating well? I'm not a cold woman. I'm not heartless. I've shown Sarah twice as much love to make up for my sins. Don't you dare come to my house and try to tell me what pain is. My whole life has been pain!"

Susan stood up from the couch and walked to the door.

"Wait," Betty called toward her, calming her tone down. "I'm just so worked up right now. Please don't tell anyone what you saw. Just one more secret. I promise it's the last one. I can't lose Will too."

Susan grabbed the handle of the door. "I won't say a thing to anyone, and I sure as hell won't be talking to you anymore either."

Slam

Betty cried for a moment, but a numb sort of rage grew within her and helped to dry her eyes. She decided that it would be a bad idea to leave a trail of bodies scattered across the woods, especially since she had just made an enemy. One body wasn't too risky, but several bodies would definitely be harder to conceal. She didn't want the risk of them being linked back to her or Will, so she came up with a better solution. She waited for Susan's car to leave, and then she walked back out to the shed. Will trailed behind her, following her inside.

"Alright Will. Remember the pigs? This is basically the same thing. Hang her up for me, can you?"

Will nodded and obeyed.

Once Ashley was in the air, dangling

upside down by a single leg, Betty handed him a knife.

"Get the rest of the blood out. It shouldn't have clotted yet."

Will sliced into Ashley's shoulders, and the rest of her blood poured out onto the floor like spilled jello. He gasped with surprise and amusement. "Just like a pig! You're right!"

Betty nodded and tried not to gag. It wasn't as exciting to her as it was to him, but she knew it had to be done. It was best to make it seem like some sort of a game to push through it. She continued shouting instructions to Will until Ashley resembled nothing more than a well-butchered pile of meat.

They took every piece out to the smoker and tossed the incriminating charred bones into a bag to be ground down and fed to the pigs at a later time.

"We'll mix the meat in with the pork until it's gone. No one will know the difference."

Tammy's fate was sealed in the same way as Ashley's, but Will had gotten lazy and tossed her bones into the woods when the grinder had jammed. He figured that Betty wouldn't notice. Unfortunately, it was his damning mistake.

Chapter 22

"With or Without You"

March 31st, 1988

Almost two years had passed since Susan last spoken to Betty. She had run into Sarah a few times during her trips into

Wintersburg, and she would smile each time she saw her wearing the lavender-colored necklace. Susan had mailed it to Sarah anonymously, and that caused a sense of mystery around the object, making her want to wear it even more. It seemed more special that way than just saying it was from a family friend. The mystery and allure turned the necklace into a treasure.

Susan didn't see Sarah on her trip this time, at least not in the flesh. Instead, she was met with a frightening poster and the faces of several missing women, pinned to a bulletin board.

"Sarah Noe," she read the name. An awful feeling, like she had been punched in the gut, took over her, and she gasped for air. Almost immediately, she ran to the payphone and dialed Betty's phone number. After two rings that seemed like two thousand, there was a voice on the line.

"Hello?"

"Betty! What happened? Sarah's missing?"

"Susan? Is that you?" Betty's voice croaked quietly.

"Of course it is! What's going on? What happened?"

"She's gone."

"What do you mean she's gone?"

"Susan. She's gone."

Betty broke into sobbing, and Susan immediately knew what she had meant. She thought of the last time they had talked. She remembered Will, his clothes dirty, his hands covered in dried blood. She recalled the smell and the alarming calmness in Betty's demeanor. That hadn't been a one-time incident. Will had killed before, and she realized that he had killed after, as well.

"Is it — did he —"

"Yes," Betty replied, her voice even more strained than before.

Shock clouded Susan's ability to react. She walked slowly to her car in the Medley's parking lot and sat down inside of it. She stared blankly ahead for a few minutes and then started the engine. She drove all the way back home to Parkington.

The sky had darkened by the time she reached the city again. She parked her car and stepped out onto the sidewalk, not even bothering to go inside at all. Her feet carried her all the way to the train tracks, about two miles from her house, and she continued staring ahead, blankly.

Many years of memories flashed around in her mind, playing back to her like a vintage film reel. She saw the highest moments of her life and the lowest. Her first love smiled and waved at her, as well as her late husband. She felt herself kiss him on the lips and then heard herself saying goodbye in a slightly younger voice. Her son's tombstone appeared as well, along with the many birthdays and Christmases that she'd spent ignoring him. She hadn't been entirely absent in his life, but she had spent his whole childhood just waiting for him to grow up. When he'd matured into a man, he surrounded himself with the people who had appreciated him and left her as only a painful memory.

Then she saw Alice, and she saw Sarah. The guilt became too much to bear.

And finally, there was a train.

Susan stepped onto the tracks as soon as she heard its whistle blowing. She walked ahead fearlessly, waiting for it to take her to a different world. In a matter of seconds, her wish came true.

***

Detective Darrow watched as one team pulled water-filled cars from the lake, and another team carried out the piles of souvenirs from the basement. With everyone assuming that Judy was still properly buried in the safety of the cemetery, only Sarah was exhumed from the crawl space. Will had been fairly cooperative over the weeks, but he wasn't going to give away any of the remaining secrets unless he was asked specifically for them. In his mind, his mother belonged exactly where he had put her. He had only tucked her into bed. Since finding out that his hair and shoe collections had been taken away as evidence, he was already upset enough.

When Sarah's remains were brought out in a body bag, Detective Darrow shivered. So much of his time and energy had gone into solving this case, and it was all being carried away in front of him. He had driven by the lake countless times since Sarah had gone missing, and she had been there waiting to be found the entire time. He wondered how many obvious clues he had missed due to time crunches, or other distractions.

Detective Darrow looked over at the large shed. He had been shielding his eyes from the scene for a while — not because it was any more gruesome than the other things, but because it was a harder reality to grasp. Murder was one thing, but what had happened in that shed was something entirely unique and disturbing. He had never even fathomed that a person could have been so sick as to dispose of bodies in such a way. His eyes wandered over to the smoker, and he grew even more nauseated as his imagination ran wild. Each time the wind blew past his face, he'd catch an unpleasant whiff of cooked meat, causing his abdomen to cramp up in ways that he'd never felt before. He could barely stand to look at the tools and the bags that were being taken out from there, but something kept him staring.

He recalled the most recent town event, and how excited Betty had been to set up her barbecue stand. With a smile on her face, she had scooped an extra portion of pulled pork onto the plates of anyone who asked for more and didn't even charge extra for it. What had seemed like an act of pure generosity to him, had actually been a smooth way for her to dispose of the evidence quickly. With no bodies to be found, she had almost gotten away with the entire thing. Will could have continued to kill, and she could have continued saving money on pigs and pig feed.

The more that Detective Darrow thought about it, the more he wished that Betty would have just left the remains in the woods. Flies and worms were meant to eat such things — people were not. Cold sweat beaded all across his skin, and his collar dampened. His face became as white as the cloth that covered the bits of bone that had been overlooked by both Betty and Will. Had they been less sloppy when feeding the useless parts to the pigs, the scene wouldn't have been such a difficult thing to be present for. The undigested teeth were the most upsetting thing for everyone to see.

On his way home, Detective Darrow drove past Alice's house. She stood on her porch, sweeping the dust away. He pulled into her driveway and parked the car. While he was a little nervous, he had been wanting to check on her for a while. Her face would hopefully be a much more welcoming sight than what he'd been dealing with all day. After all, anything would have probably been better than that. He wiped the remaining nervous sweat from his face and stepped out into the cool air once more. He walked up toward the porch, trying to appear confident and unphased.

"Hey, Alice. Nice day out, isn't it?"

"Yeah, I guess it is, actually. What brings you over here? I thought you guys were digging today."

He nodded, and quickly changed the subject. That was the last thing he wanted to talk about. "We are. I just wanted to see how you were doing or if you needed anything. I heard from Roger that you were thinking about moving back to Parkington."

"Actually, about that — I did some

more thinking and I'm planning on staying here in town for a while instead."

"Really?" he replied, surprised. "I figured that you would already be packing up your things by now."

"It crossed my mind. I won't lie about that, but there's something keeping me here. I really can't explain it, and I'd feel like a crazy person if I tried to put it into words. It just feels like home, you know? Despite everything."

"Well, honestly, I can't say I understand. I'm just glad you'll still be nearby though."

Alice laughed lightly. "You don't need to understand it. I really hardly understand it myself. I just know that this feels right. Roger even told me not to worry about the rent for a while, too, which is also a plus."

Detective Darrow was happy to see that Alice seemed a lot like her usual self. He was well aware of her mask though. "Yeah, I had a long talk with him after we took Betty in. We didn't think she was going to survive for a while. Roger was an absolute mess. I think he really blames himself for not seeing any of the signs. None of us saw them though. I mean, even I'm still in shock from the whole thing."

"You know, it's funny. He left this

necklace and a letter on my porch the other day. He wrote something about it being more mine than his and told me to take care of it. I don't even know how he knew I was interested in it." She lifted Sarah's necklace from beneath the collar of her shirt and held onto it by the pendant. "I thought I'd only told Tiffany about this."

"That's interesting. What's so special about it?"

"Probably nothing really, other than it was Sarah's. Initially, I thought it looked like something my grandma wore in her old photos, but I think I was just trying to piece every odd thing in this town together at the time."

Detective Darrow nodded and smiled. "You're probably right. At least it's pretty though. Sarah would probably be happy to know that it's being taken care of."

"You're right. She'd probably like that someone was wearing it, instead of just having it left in a drawer somewhere." Alice returned his smile. "Would you like to come in? I can make us some coffee if you'd like."

"I'd like that a lot actually."

Detective Darrow followed Alice inside. And there, he stayed, protecting her. He knew that years flew by as quickly as flies flew out from a hot shed and that Benji would be out of prison in no time at all. While the true murderers would be spending their entire lives behind bars, he knew that evil was always nearby, just waiting for its chance to pounce.

E. H. Night is a fan of Mysteries and Thrillers, which are both reflected in her writing. She tries to find light in even the darkest of situations. Aside from writing, she can often be found painting or spending time with her family.

Made in the USA
San Bernardino, CA
12 November 2019